Penguin Books
Kingsley's Touch

John Collee was born in 1955 and educated at George Watson's College, Edinburgh. A year of his childhood was spent in India. He studied medicine at the University of Edinburgh and subsequently practised in Cambridge, Bristol and Bath. He was Radio Bristol's phone-in doctor before moving to London to take up a scriptwriting post with the BBC. He now divides his time between medicine and writing. *Kingsley's Touch* is his first novel.

G000147448

John Collee

Kingsley's Touch

Penguin Books

Penguin Books Ltd, Harmondsworth, Middlesex, England
Viking Penguin Inc., 40 West 23rd Street, New York, New York 10010, U.S.A.
Penguin Books Australia Ltd, Ringwood, Victoria, Australia
Penguin Books Canada Ltd, 2801 John Street, Markham, Ontario, Canada L3R 1B4
Penguin Books (N.Z.) Ltd, 182–190 Wairau Road, Auckland 10, New Zealand

First published by Allen Lane 1984
Published in Penguin Books 1985

Made and printed in Great Britain by
Hazell Watson & Viney Limited,
Member of the BPCC Group,
Aylesbury, Bucks
Set in VIP Palatino

1

It was the kind of street to which all the ragged derelicts of the town eventually descended. Few people therefore paid much attention to the gaunt, wild-eyed Indian who barged between them. And Acharya Dhangi, sunken-cheeked with exhaustion, was in turn too preoccupied to notice. There was something about this street . . . a strange familiarity.

The one o'clock hooter sounded from the docks and a verse from the *shruti* sprang to his mind:

> *Thus you will know Nigambodh Ghat*
> *The black waters lick at its steps*
> *Black with the blood of the sons of Pandu*
> *Of Subhadra and the sons of Draupadi*
> *And the great conch Pandra smites the heavens.*

Strangers seemed to clog the pavement in front of him and the tired leather suitcase became more frequently ensnared between them. But even as he wrenched it free their protests went unheeded. So intent was he on making headway that the Douglas Calder, set back as it was from the shop-fronts, took him by surprise.

Dhangi stopped. At first he thought it was not the place, just another old Victorian hospital in black stone, the forecourt cluttered with recent extensions, to the right the X-ray department, to the left the outpatients. And yet, on closer inspection, he realized that this hospital had its past lives like any man. The original building had been quite symmetrical: four storeys with a tower at each corner.

Still clutching his suitcase, Dhangi broke into an awkward

run along the front of the hospital. He could not remember the last time he had eaten and this burst of extra effort seemed to drain the strength from his legs. His feet fell heavily on the cobbles as he turned down Causeway Lane. Now he could see the harbour in front of him.

> . . . *the black waters lick at its steps*
> *Black with the blood of the sons of Pandu* . . .

A covey of gulls left the discarded chip packet they had been scavenging and took to the air in front of him, hoisting their white bodies skywards to disappear, crying, over the blank side wall of the hospital.

Dhangi turned another corner. An expanse of cobbles separated the back of the hospital from the water's edge, but access to it was barred by an iron gate. Dhangi tried to force his head between the railings but could not get a satisfactory view. Breathing heavily he flung the suitcase over in front of him and scaled the low wall. A spike penetrated the worn sole of one shoe as he clambered over the railings but Dhangi did not feel it. With a supreme effort he hauled his emaciated body to the top and jumped to the ground, landing heavily on the other side. As he rose to his feet his heart was leaping in his throat, a great roar sounding in his ears. He retrieved his suitcase and stumbled backwards to the waterfront. As he did so the massive black façade of Nigambodh Ghat unfolded before him, the grey storm-clouds piled above it. Dhangi filled his lungs and let out a long, keening cry of victory.

Cranley wheezed, ground out a cigarette and unlocked the door with the dour concentration he applied to all his work. Above him, in the wedge of darkening sky between anaesthetics and the mortuary, the dockland gulls wheeled and called. Cranley stopped and squinted northwards. The vanguard of the storm was already sweeping over the Firth of Forth. Sheets of distant rain draped the sky behind the harbour wall. But he was looking at a figure in the foreground, a dark man in a white shirt sitting near the harbour's edge with his back to the hospital. Now, above the abrasive cries of the gulls, Cranley could discern a new sound: the man's voice. Chanting.

Cranley left the mortuary door unlocked and backed down the steps. He cleared his sinuses and spat against the hospital wall. The cobbled wharf was hospital property and Cranley made it his business to find out about anyone trespassing there. As he approached, the chanting became more distinct. It was a foreign language which Cranley did not recognize. Cranley emerged on to the courtyard. His irregular stride quickened in tempo.

'Hoy!' he shouted.

Dhangi's eyes were closed but his mind was filled with a vibrating light of searing intensity. Kundalini the serpent braced the six *chakras* of his spine. From somewhere beyond the massive grey sky above the Firth of Forth energy rushed through him, was focused beyond him. His jacket lay by his side but he felt no cold. Divine grace flowed through his limbs like honey. He was *Brahman*. He was one with the universe.

Cranley came closer. In front of the cross-legged Indian a few dried flower petals flapped like trapped butterflies from the surface of the bollard, sticking to something that looked suspiciously like blood.

'Hoy,' he shouted again.

A dark flaw appeared in the crystal of Dhangi's consciousness and flared outwards. The light flickered and dimmed. Kundalini stirred in his spine. Dhangi's eyes opened.

'What the hell are you up to?'

It took some time after achieving *samadhi* for his mind to accommodate language. Dhangi turned, still cross-legged, and looked upwards. The old mortuary assistant towered over him, his face a landscape of disgust and incredulity. Dhangi groped for an English word of dismissal and failed to encounter

9

one. He remained silent and felt for his suitcase. As he did so it landed on his lap and he was yanked upwards by his collar.

'Take your hands off me.' The words came from some previously shuttered part of Dhangi's brain and he had shouted them before consciously formulating the phrase. Now he was on his feet, the case in his hand, trembling with cold and emotion.

Cranley had taken a pace back, momentarily shocked by the violence of the stranger's reaction. He rallied quickly. 'Come on. Hop it!'

Dhangi bent stiffly and picked up his jacket. The religious ecstasy was sliding from his mind, leaving behind great scars of resentment. Cranley jerked his head towards the hospital and Dhangi followed him in that direction. When they reached the mortuary Cranley hobbled up the steps and opened the door. Dhangi paused and looked up, taking in the tiled white anteroom with its regiment of boots and aprons. Cranley stepped deliberately sideways, blocking his line of vision.

'I am a doctor,' Dhangi volunteered.

Cranley cleared his sinuses and looked the stranger over, assessing at a glance the soiled shirt, the frayed cuffs and the crumpled black shoes. In twenty years at the Douglas Calder he'd seen vagrants of just about every description. This one was further gone than most.

'You're no doctor, pal,' he said.

'I hope to be taking up a position here.'

Cranley snorted. 'I'll tell you the position you'll get – flat on your back, outside these gates. Got it?'

A brief look of intense hatred flickered across Dhangi's hollowed face, then he turned and moved off down the alleyway and into the hospital's front car park. Cranley watched him go, then stepped into the mortuary and snibbed the door behind him. The first angry gusts of wind were rattling the skylight as he took off the black gaberdine and hung it on a peg. Before removing his shoes he performed a neat manoeuvre with the back of his tongue, dislodging his false teeth and pushing them to the front of his mouth. Then he took out a handkerchief and began to polish the ivories, grimly delighted with his own rhetorical inventiveness.

2

The storm was almost upon them now. From the hospital's second floor Alistair Kingsley looked down critically on the fantastic mismatch of the Douglas Calder: smoke-blackened stone, slate and turret, lodged like a decaying tooth in the dockland's commercial centre.

The Indian was still there.

'What do you think he's up to?'

McReady squeezed up alongside. There wasn't much room in the nursing station and Sister McReady's displacement was considerable. 'Who?'

'That coloured chap beside the statue.'

'Don't know,' said Sister McReady. 'We didn't get clairvoyance when I was at nursing school. Probably someone's boyfriend.'

'Glad he's not mine,' said Kingsley.

'Well, I wouldn't worry yourself about him.' Sister McReady squeezed past again and straightened her pleats. 'Some boozer – he's not doing any harm.'

She was right: Leith was full of oddballs.

'Where's the Spears girl?' he asked.

Whenever he entered the ward all heads would turn towards him in supplication. Days like today he felt swamped. He was a consultant surgeon, not the Pope. Halfway down the ward Sandra Spears was sitting up in bed. She lowered her magazine. Kingsley smiled at her and McReady pulled the screens around them both. He looked out of the window. From behind the hospital, like some celestial demolition, came the first distant peal of thunder.

'Just take that off, will you?'

Sandra Spears lifted the nightgown over her head and shook her hair. Her breasts fell forwards, fat and firm skinned.

A flush began at the base of her neck and crept down her cleavage. Sister McReady stood sentry with her jaw on one side. Kingsley surveyed the curve of his patient's bosom, his voice was level, pragmatic, reassuring.

'Pop your hands on your head.' With the flat of his fingers he touched her right breast.

'How old are you?'

'Thirty-two,' she said.

'Do you work?'

'No.'

'Your husband.'

'Yes . . . I mean he's a journalist.' She shivered.

'Sorry, is my hand cold?' he asked.

Kingsley was working around the breast, his long fingers in the soft tissue. The first drops of rain slapped against the window. Outside, the bus queue bunched under the shelter like some sensitive crustacean.

'You noticed it two weeks ago.'

'Yes. In the bath.'

'Do you get painful breasts with your periods?'

'No, well sometimes.'

'What did Mr Jennings tell you?'

'He said it might be . . . it might be . . .'

Kingsley glanced at her face. Her lips were compressed, her eyes damp. He moved to the left side. He could feel, below his exploring hand, the bounding of her heartbeat. McReady lumbered round to be next to her. McReady must have been a great mother – a formidable wife but a great mother.

'How many children do you have, Sandra?'

'Three,' his patient told him.

'How big's the eldest?'

'Ah . . . ten.'

Over the top of his spectacles, Kingsley awarded her one of his rare smiles. He remembered Sheila at this age. Then found it — a hard mass in the axillary tail. The size of a marble.

'Can you put your hands on your hips?'

Sandra Spears looked at his face.

He rolled the mass. His fingers compressed, coaxed it. Above the noise of the rain on the skylight there came another muttering of thunder. Closer now.

He avoided the question in her gaze. The lump was not attached to muscle, but it did have the craggy feel of a cancer. Something else: where he touched it there was a feeling of heat which was outside his normal experience. He took his hand away, looked at the skin, then placed his hand on the mass. The same thing, warmth. Kingsley put his hand on his own cheek. It worried him that his senses might be deceiving him. He relied on sight and touch, above all touch. He frowned.

'Mr Kingsley?' Sandra Spears's voice was thin with apprehension. She read his expression. It said cancer. Kingsley had been her last hope. She began to cry, silently at first, then she drew up her knees and pressed her fingers in her eyes, elbows covering her naked, vulnerable breasts. Kingsley patted her knee.

'Hey, come on,' he said, 'it's wet enough already.'

Outside, the rain had increased in intensity. It fell on the Co-op, the cobbles, the muddy, wheezing buses. It fell on the hospital roofs, overflowing the ancient runnels and glossing the tiles. A notice on the railings had said 'Save the Douglas Calder'. It was now illegible. Kingsley's voice continued, rational, cajoling.

'. . . no need to fear the worst. I won't tell you it's not cancer. You're the right age . . . but an early first pregnancy is a point in your favour . . .'

'. . . might be a cyst . . . a piece of dead fat . . .'

Still her shoulders juddered. McReady gave her a tissue.

'You know the plan,' said Kingsley. 'Friday we remove the lump. If it's malignant we go on and take the breast as well.' She looked at him. 'Gives you the best chance of a cure,' he said.

She nodded. Kingsley patted her shoulder. They left her with the screens still round, protection against the emotional pawnbrokers on the ward.

Back in the office McReady was getting stroppy. 'You're not putting her on Friday.'

'I am.'

'What – with Niven and the two others? You'll be wanting to work on the Sabbath next.'

'Yes,' said Kingsley. 'Unfortunately it's impossible to get theatre staff.'

'You'll be working yourself to an early grave, Mr Kingsley.'

'I thought they didn't teach you clairvoyance.'

McReady's mouth set like a vice. Kingsley put an arm around her shoulder. 'I've a waiting list as long as your belt. If I could get through them all working a thirty-hour week, I'd be a happy man.'

'Fiddlesticks.' McReady put her fists in her pockets. 'You'd be out there canvassing for more patients.'

'I'm told it's my Presbyterian sense of duty.'

'Duty's got nothing to do with it – you just like operating.'

'That's true as well,' said Kingsley. He couldn't argue with McReady. He'd known her too long.

He wandered through the Barton ward with his chin on his chest and his hands in his pockets. It would be less harrowing with Mr Niven.

'You see that statue?' he commented as the patient dropped his pyjama trousers. 'Douglas Calder. He founded this place. Campaigned all his life against disease and immorality. Died of syphilis. Pop up on the bed, would you?'

Niven was already familiar with the routine for examination.

15

He lay on his side and brought his knees up to his chest. Kingsley slipped on a glove.

'I'm just going to feel up your back passage.'

Jennings had been right about Niven too. Almost filling the rectum there was an ugly granular mass.

The light was already beginning to fail. Kingsley cast his eyes around the car park below. At first he thought the stranger had gone.

'OK, Mr Niven, you can roll back now.' But as Kingsley was straightening, something through the swimming, rattling window caught his eye. A figure had moved in the doorway of X-ray below him. Hands in his jacket pockets. The Indian stranger. Waiting.

As he finally closed his office the great mahogany clock was striking six. Visiting hour had made an aviary of the entrance hall. These were the inhabitants of Edinburgh's dockland – swaddled in wool, hauling kids, rattling the coffee dispenser. On the last chime they began to swarm up the stairs. Kingsley walked towards the door and they parted before him. William was on duty at the door, hair sprouting from his ears and nose like stuffing, a blue mammal in a glass case.

Outside Kingsley raised his brolly. Halfway across the car park he became aware of the footsteps. He ignored them, headed for his car, rattled the keys in the door, threw his suitcase in the back and switched on the headlights.

Then he looked up.

The stranger stood in front of the bonnet, his face illuminated from below like an actor in some Victorian burlesque. He walked around the car. Kingsley hesitated, cursed and rolled down the window. Some rain came in.

'Mr Kingsley.'

'Yes.'

'I am Dr Dhangi.'

Had they ever met before? Kingsley had no recollection of

the face that bent towards him, the dark brows, the crudely chopped hair and inflamed eyes. Rationally he should have felt repelled by the stranger; a strong, damp smell was emanating from his clothes and his breath reeked of betel. But for one unguarded moment Kingsley was aware of an uncanny surge of kinship – a forcing in the chest which he could only relate to the sensation he experienced on meeting Sheila after long separations. The sensation disturbed him and he retreated into formality. 'Do I know you?'

Dhangi was staring at him with feverish intensity. 'You do.'

'I think you're mistaken.' Kingsley made to roll up the window.

'No. Please. You must listen.' There was a peculiar authority to the Indian's quick, nervous speech. Almost involuntarily Kingsley released the window handle.

Dhangi faltered. 'I have prayed for this moment.'

The confession restored Kingsley's powers of resistance. 'Look,' he said, 'I don't know what you're talking about. Is there something you want?'

'We must talk.'

'I really don't think that's . . .'

'You must give me a job . . .' the Indian interjected. '. . . A job,' he repeated, desperately rummaging in the inside pocket of his jacket. 'I am a doctor, a pathologist. I must enter your employment. I have a number of references from my university . . .'

In the twilight Kingsley saw Dhangi produce what looked like a thick brown envelope which he now attempted to push into the car. The address of Jalore University Medical School was stamped on one corner. Kingsley refused to take it. He was back in familiar territory. 'Please, Dr Dhangi,' he remonstrated, 'I appreciate your enthusiasm but quite frankly this is neither the time nor the place for a job interview. I've had a very tiring day and I'm keen to get home and put my feet up. If you want to make an appointment you can contact my secretary.'

17

'Your secretary,' Dhangi repeated blankly.

'Yes. Goodbye now.' Kingsley looked pointedly at Dhangi's free hand which was still resting on the car window.

Dhangi hesitated, standing half bent in the pouring rain in an embarrassing limbo of indecision. Then, decided, he said, 'Yes . . . till later then,' and offered his hand to shake.

Kingsley twisted sideways and raised his own, but the Indian did not grasp it. Instead he ran one finger lightly along one side of the palm, uttering as he did so a strangled gasp of recognition. Kingsley recoiled and briskly wound up the window. He took his foot off the clutch and the car lurched forwards. The jolt helped him regain his composure. Kingsley nosed out of the hospital car park, turning right into the glut of traffic. When he glanced in the rear-view mirror the Indian was nowhere to be seen. Dhangi had prostrated himself on the soaking, filthy hospital quadrangle. Now, inaudible and unnoticed, he raised his head from the ground, extending his red-stained palms to the heavens:

> *Dharma Ayurveda*
> *Through this man*
> *You will touch all beings*
> *In yourself*
> *And also in me*

Like Cranley, Kingsley was a man of habit but tonight he did not take his usual route home: the slow drag up Leith Walk to Princes Street. Instead he turned left at the Mecca bingo. A narrow cobbled crescent brought him out on Ferry Road. As he headed westwards the black tenements fell away, the pavements broadened.

Two miles further on he turned left again, down the wide boulevard that transects Inverleith park. Driving south now he could see, above the trees, the lights and spires of his old school. Kingsley had spent a long time in this town. But even now, as the hospital to which he had devoted the last decade was threatened with closure, he had no desire to leave. He was happy here, cemented into this buttress of the medical profession. He knew that it was the stability of men like himself which sustained the profession. Just as it was the profession which sustained men like himself.

Rejoining the traffic in Stockbridge he climbed up through the shambles of mews houses where he had lived as a student. He had already dismissed Dhangi from his thoughts. His mind had returned, as it would always return, to his work. He was thinking of Mr Niven. There had been something odd about the feel of Niven's bowel cancer – like Spears's breast lump, that uncanny sensation of warmth.

3

White tiled floor, white walls, hot white light. Sandra Spears's white breast, adrift in a sea of green drapes, rose and fell with her breathing.

'OK to cut, Richard?'

A nurse tic-tacked across the floor bundling the drapes from a previous operation. Kingsley felt for the mass. It was less easily palpable than he remembered but he could still identify it – a discrete nodule in the tail of the breast. Overlying the lump there was a barely perceptible reddening of the skin. He hadn't noticed that before. He checked the skin creases, then stretched the skin between finger and thumb. The knife performed a neat ellipse. Jennings, his registrar, dabbed the blood.

Richard Short lifted his gold digital watch off the anaesthetic trolley and squinted at it critically. If this one was malignant he could add a forty-minute mastectomy to the list. That took them to half past three. Then the hemicolectomy. So much for his squash court.

This present anaesthetic was a doddle. Even the bowel resection seemed unlikely to prove taxing. Short yawned and stroked his moustaches. Routine anaesthesia bored him to death. He glanced at his assistant and mentally sketched in the contour suggested by her theatre pyjamas.

Kingsley spoke without looking up. 'How was your holiday?'

'Bloody marvellous. It's been pissing ever since I got back.'

'Good fishing weather . . . diathermy please,' said Kingsley. He buzzed the small bleeders and they retracted, cauterized, into the subcutaneous fat.

Richard Short looked up. His face appeared over the horizon of Sandra Spears's breast.

'Babcocks,' said Kingsley. A Babcocks forceps slapped into his hand.

'I've never understood the attraction of fishing,' said Short.

'You have to be committed to go out in this.'

Short looked at the drizzle on the window. 'You ought to be committed if you go out in that.'

But then, he reflected, Kingsley was. He watched the surgeon grab the suspicious section in forceps and cut it free from the surrounding tissue. Kingsley did two or three of these operations every week. Had done for years. What sustained his interest? Commitment? Probably Sheila was right – the Presbyterian upbringing. Short himself had been raised on money and cynicism in equal parts. Sometimes he envied Kingsley's contentment.

Under the drapes Sandra Spears's breathing continued, slow and regular. The breast rose and fell.

Kingsley looked down at his friend and caught him yawning. 'What you need, Richard, is a game of golf.'

But Short could not muster enthusiasm even for his consuming passion. 'Greens are like paddy fields.'

'Small artery forceps,' said Kingsley. The ratchet rang as he clamped them shut. 'We've been golfing in the rain before.'

'Madness,' said Short. 'You just couldn't bear to let me win the hospital cup by default.'

Short's assistant was opening vials with the casual competence of a farmer's daughter cracking eggs. Right now he didn't need a game of golf. On St Lucia he'd been able to identify what he really needed – regular sex.

'Saturday week,' said Kingsley, 'two pounds a stroke.'

'Weather permitting,' said Richard Short. It had never ceased to amaze him how Scotsmen in general, and Kingsley in particular, constructed religions from their hobbies. If Hurricane Alma hit Scotland the weekend golfers would still be out there, dodging the flying gorse bushes and driving into the wind.

'Right, specimen pot. Are pathology expecting this?'

The houseman confirmed that they were.

'OK, chromic, swab, needle . . .' said Kingsley.

'. . . coffee, milk,' said Short. He relinquished his stool to his assistant.

'If you want anything . . .'

'. . . just whistle,' she said.

'. . . just . . . yes, am I getting predictable?' He patted her on the bottom.

Kingsley stood for a moment as his registrar began to close the wound. He hoped they wouldn't have to proceed further. Mastectomy was a mutilation, something he would rather not inflict on a young woman like Sandra Spears. He pulled off his mask and followed the anaesthetist.

In the rest room, Richard Short rummaged in the wall cupboard for the powdered milk he could never find. Kingsley sat heavily on one of the fibre-glass chairs.

'Feeling a bit peaky, Alistair?'

Kingsley looked in the mirror. The inscription 'Hollister Colostomy Bags' superimposed itself on his forehead. 'Funny thing, these last three days, every time I come into the hospital I get . . .'

'Don't tell me, I know the feeling.'

'I'm being serious.'

'So am I.'

Kingsley squeezed the back of his own neck. 'Ever since that character approached me in the car park.'

'Bad vibes is what we call it.'

'It's not what *I* call it,' said Kingsley. 'I think he's given me the flu. Sheila tells me it's the male menopause.'

'Ha!' Richard Short found the milk. 'Sure she isn't just suggesting you should fuck her more often?'

Kingsley cast his eyes heavenwards. Much as he liked Short,

there were times when the man took his contemporary image too far. Kingsley went to a locker and rummaged for the pipe in the pocket of his tweeds. He loaded it in silence.

Richard Short picked up a copy of the *British Medical Journal* and scanned the list of contents on its cover.

' "Ten cases of phaeochromocytoma associated with medullary carcinoma of the thyroid" – who writes this stuff?'

Kingsley drew on the tobacco. 'It's a good article that.'

'You mean you've read it?' Short was genuinely astounded.

'Yes,' said Kingsley. 'You might find it relevant.'

'You're talking to the man who fell asleep during *Jaws*,' Short told him, 'and that was a damn sight less boring than this stuff. I wouldn't get past the first paragraph.'

'Have you tried?'

Short threw the magazine back at the table. 'Come on, Alistair, it's small print.'

'I always read the small print,' said Kingsley.

The phone rang. Kingsley answered it immediately, but it was not pathology.

'Take this frozen section,' he continued. 'Half a dozen cells down the microscope. Can't get much smaller than that. Right now it's the most important thing in Sandra Spears's life.'

Short reached for another magazine. 'I was talking about phaeochromocytoma. Tits are different . . . ah! *Cosmopolitan*, that's more like it.'

Kingsley smiled and said nothing. He knew when he was being goaded.

Twenty minutes later the phone rang again. This time it was the pathologist.

'Dr Mukesh here, pathology. About this specimen, Spears, Sandra Spears, I don't think I've seen anything like this before . . .'

'You don't have to shout, Mukesh, I'm not senile yet.'

'Sorry, sir.'

'And try not to talk so fast,' said Kingsley.

'No. Sorry. Yes, very strange indeed. Lots of abnormal cells and many many mitotic figures . . .'

'Malignant,' said Kingsley.

'Well, yes, sir; what puzzles me is there's some kind of reaction going on at the periphery. As you know, we normally expect a mild degree of inflammation . . . but not this . . .'

'Not what?'

'Well it is incredible; there are areas where the disease is almost walled off by white cells.' Mukesh cleared his throat.

'Was it infiltrating?' Kingsley asked.

'Well yes, in parts . . . at least it had been.'

'Are you wanting to take more sections?'

'Don't see it's going to tell us any more, Mr Kingsley.'

'So it's malignant.' Kingsley looked to Short and put his hand to his head.

'Well, what I'm saying,' Mukesh continued, 'is the host seems to be setting up some kind of reaction. She appears almost to be overcoming the cancer.'

'Impossible.'

'Quite agree, at least so one would have thought.'

'I'm telling you, Dr Mukesh. It's impossible.'

'Well, yes.'

'So we cut,' said Kingsley.

There was silence on the other end of the phone. 'We need a decision, Dr Mukesh. I'm not going to stop here. Removing the lump will have seeded cancer cells throughout the breast. I don't want to tell you your job, but mitotic figures plus infiltration equals cancer. No? And that means mastectomy.'

'I suppose that's right.'

'I'm sure of it; you'll tell me about the paraffin sections?' Kingsley put the phone down and knocked out his pipe.

'What was all that about?' Richard Short was already tying his mask.

'Oh, the new pathologist. Some rare variant he's discovered.'

'Important?'

'Small print.'

'*Touché.*'

Kingsley smiled wryly. 'Cancer though.' He stood up.

Richard Short dropped the magazine. 'Another bloody marathon.'

Sheila Kingsley moved the rubber plant to get a better view of herself. She rather liked the effect. She slapped her tummy and turned round to check the back view. Kingsley was sitting up in bed. He looked at her over the top of his glasses.

'What's that?'

'It's a leotard. You've seen leotards before,' she told him.

'Now you mention it,' said Kingsley, '*Top of the Pops*?'

She was not being drawn.

'Strange thing to wear in bed,' he said.

'I'm not going to wear it in bed.'

'Why d'you put it on then?'

'For my yoga.'

Kingsley undid the top button of his pyjamas and settled down behind the *British Journal of Surgery*.

She sat upright on the floor, concentrating on her breathing. From Kingsley's viewpoint the lower half of her body was obscured by the foot of the bed.

'When did you take up yoga?'

She didn't look at him. 'I'm going to teach my nine-year-olds how to do it.'

Kingsley returned to his journal. After a while he looked up again.

'What does that do?'

'Relaxation – it balances the conflicting forces of Yin and Yang.'

'What's Yin and Yang?'

'They're body forces.'

'How do you know, has anyone measured them?'

'Oh for God's sake, Alistair.'

Kingsley consulted his journal again. Sheila continued her yoga on the carpet. After fifteen minutes she left to take a shower. When she came back to bed he moved over. Her legs were cold. Kingsley was still absorbed in his reading. Sheila picked up a book and put it down. She rolled over and put her chin on his chest.

'What are you reading about?'

'Well it's all a bit technical,' said Kingsley evasively. Then he lowered the magazine. 'Do you want to talk?'

'No,' she lied.

Kingsley settled into the pillows. 'Richard reckons I should make love to you more often.'

She sat up. 'Well there's nothing like bandying your private life about at work.'

'No, he just said it as a joke.'

'I see; you said, "Sheila's getting a bit frisky these days" and Richard looked round from whoever you were operating on at the time and said "Well, Alistair old chap, the thing to do is fuck her more often".'

'No, it wasn't like that.'

'So what was it like?'

'Oh come on, I just said I'd been feeling off colour, and you know how Richard is, he said . . .'

'He said, "Well there's nothing so good for you as humping".'

Kingsley looked at her despairingly. She knew he found that kind of thing offensive. He replaced his spectacles and picked up his journal. Sheila remained sitting. Eventually he put a hand on her bare back. 'Well, would you rather . . .'

She observed a diplomatic silence.

'. . . rather make love more often?'

'More often than what?'

Kingsley unbuttoned his jacket and caught her round the

waist. 'Come here,' he said. She gave a little yelp. They sank under the quilt and her legs twined round his.

'It's all right, darling,' she said as his hands found her buttocks. 'Don't feel you have to comply with every bizarre little whim . . . There is the age difference. You can't be too careful. Maybe I should take a younger lover . . . or Richard could help out . . . how would that suit you . . . then while I'm screwing you can read . . . that . . . that whatever it was . . . ah, that's rather nice.'

Then the phone rang.

It had rung three times, when Sheila pulled away.

'Not important,' said Kingsley.

'Mightn't it be an emergency?'

'Better be.' Kingsley raised his head and disentangled himself, pulling his pyjamas across his erection. He took the receiver. 'Hello.'

A coin dropped. The voice was slightly slurred and louder than was necessary.

'Is that Mr Alistair Kingsley?'

'It is.'

'Roland Spears.'

'Hello, is this vitally important?'

'It is to me.' The voice was suddenly abrasive.

Kingsley wondered who Roland Spears was.

'I just wanted to ask you.' The voice broke, resumed at a more even pitch. 'I just wanted to ask you about the operation on my wife.'

'You're Sandra Spears's husband . . .'

Roland Spears's breathing was deep and rapid.

Kingsley continued: '. . . well, as you will no doubt have been told, the, the mass was malignant, so, as you will appreciate, it was necessary to perform a mastectomy.'

'That's not what I heard.'

'I'm sorry?'

'I heard there was some doubt about the specimen you took.'

Kingsley supported himself on one elbow. He released Sheila's wrist. 'I'm sorry, Mr Spears, I don't know where you got hold of this information. There was no doubt. The cells were malignant.'

'That's not what I heard.'

'Mr Spears, why don't you ring me in the morning and we'll talk this one over . . .'

'Don't patronize me, Kingsley. Strikes me there are times you characters take your professional objectivity too . . .'

'You've had a few to drink, Mr Spears. You may regret saying this in the morning.'

'Listen, you bastard.' Spears was suddenly yelling down the phone. 'You cut off my wife's breast without waiting for a second opinion. For all you know that could have been a bum lab. report.'

'I have the utmost confidence in Dr Mukesh.'

'Well I don't have any fucking confidence in either of you.'

'I don't have to listen to this,' said Kingsley quietly.

'I'll tell you what you don't have, Kingsley. You don't have a wife with one breast.'

Kingsley's hand shook as he put down the receiver.

'Who was that?'

'Someone's husband.'

'What did he want?'

'I don't want to talk about it just now.' He kissed her on the forehead.

'Alistair?'

No response.

She turned over and lay facing him.

Kingsley put his hands behind his head and looked at the ceiling.

4

'I wouldn't go in there if I was you, Dr Short.'

Kingsley's secretary looked up at him. She was biting the end of a Biro, lips half parted. In between paperwork Rhona spent a lot of time rehearsing the physical vocabulary of her trade: for example this raising of the eyebrows, legs tightly crossed, free foot angled downwards. At times she would groom the middle finger of her left hand, or, as Kingsley paused for dictation, perform elegant, languorous preening movements with one elbow on her knee.

'I just wanted to remind him about the game.'

The rain had abated over the past few days. Now a watery sun sneaked over the crow-step gables.

'Golf?' said Rhona. 'I'll tell him later. He's had a bad morning.'

'What, in theatre?'

'No, something that happened after that.'

'Tell him he's working too hard,' said Short.

'I do.' She smiled sweetly.

Short tore his eyes away from the taut linen curve of her bosom and focused instead on the delicate smile lines at the corners of her mouth. There was something unnervingly crisp about Rhona. From the perfectly aligned seams of her stockings to the unruffled mane of blonde hair she dressed with almost puritanical precision. Hence the speculative rumour amongst most of the middle-grade registrars that the area between her legs was frequently powdered but little used. Short found this concept consistently challenging.

'How was your holiday?' she was asking.

'A continuous romp.'

'Certainly looks like an expensive tan.'

'It is extensive.'

'I said expensive.'

'Yes, that too; shall I put you down for a private viewing?'

'You can't shock me, Dr Short.'

He often wondered about that. Her highly polished manner evoked in him a recurring urge to take her manicured hand and plunge it down the front of his trousers. Kingsley shouted her name. Richard Short winked and left. Rhona stepped through the communicating door.

She found Kingsley pacing the space in front of his desk. At intervals he dragged a hand through his hair. His mouth was tight with anger. 'I don't suppose you've read this.'

Rhona sat down and smoothed her skirt. 'It's a pathology report,' she volunteered.

'I know what it is,' he snapped. 'Listen to this: "Niven . . . A.P. resection, Friday the fifth . . . carcinoma of the rectum . . . Blah blah." ' He scanned down to the relevant section, then read again with renewed hostility: ' ". . . extraordinary finding . . . the carcinoma had obviously undergone an acute inflammatory change . . . lymphocytic infiltration . . . macrophages apparently engulfing tumour . . . I personally have only seen, indeed heard of, one similar such microscopic appearance – that of the 'breast tumour' removed from Sandra Spears on the same day . . . " ' Kingsley slammed the report flat on his desk, knocking the phone receiver.

' "Breast tumour," he says, "breast tumour", inverted commas.'

Rhona pursed her lips around her pen and leant forwards on the writing-pad.

'I mean if I can't rely on the pathologist's support . . .' Kingsley dragged the seat out from his desk, then decided not to sit down. She had seen him like this six months previously when they first threatened to close the hospital.

'Get me Mukesh on the phone.'

'Don't you think you should just write a note, Mr Kingsley?'

'No I do not.'

She raised an eyebrow. Behind Kingsley, on the panelled wall, there was a Geigy calendar showing pictures of the Scottish Highlands. September was Eilan Donan castle.

Kingsley sat down. He removed his spectacles and pressed the ball of a thumb in his eye socket. 'OK, take this down. I want it to be sent over today, now . . . To Dr C. Mukesh, Department of Pathology.

'Dear Dr Mukesh.' Kingsley sat back in the leather chair and scowled at the ceiling, '. . . thanks for your interesting reports on Spears . . . ah, 632874 . . . and Niven . . . look up his reference number . . .

'. . . I can think of no explanation for these appearances short of your own . . . no scrub that . . . short of some technical artefact. I think we can ignore them.

'. . . new paragraph. I would just like to say that on Friday I was put in a very embarrassing position by Mrs Spears's husband who, unknown to me, had been given access to what is essentially a confidential report. I'd like to make quite clear that . . .'

The phone interrupted him. Kingsley picked it up himself.

'Mr Kingsley, I've been wanting to speak to you.'

'Mukesh, yes. I've been wanting to speak to you too.'

Kingsley's voice was a brick wall. Chandra Mukesh stopped dead.

'I'll get this out of my system,' said the consultant. He looked at his secretary. She was stroking her cheek with a fingernail. 'I've just been dictating a letter which is a good deal more polite than it could have been.'

'Oh?'

'Basically it's simple etiquette. I don't expect to have to justify my decisions to the relatives of patients . . .' His voice was rising. He checked himself. '. . . Someone told Spears's husband she didn't have cancer.'

'Yes . . . yes, he phoned and asked me. I thought he had a right to know. All I said was . . .'

'Well I don't think he has any damn right to know. Not from you anyway . . .'

There was a long hiatus. Kingsley wished the other man would offer some word of apology so he in turn could absolve him. Mukesh offered no cue.

'You wanted to tell me something,' said Kingsley flatly.

Mukesh paused, embarrassed, then: 'Well, it's just the testicular tumour you removed this morning . . . it's the same . . . lot of dead cells.'

'Listen, Dr Mukesh. I appreciate your enthusiasm. How long have you been a senior registrar?'

'Two months.'

'Why don't you send a couple of these specimens up to the Royal for a second opinion?' Kingsley chewed a finger. He was wondering how he would stand with the journalist Spears if Mukesh had made a mistake.

'The lower pole of that testicle was visibly necrotic, Mr Kingsley.'

'Do you think I don't know a necrotic cancer when I see one.'

'I'm sorry, sir.'

Kingsley hung up.

Rhona gave him her look.

'You think I was unfair.'

Rhona licked an envelope and sealed it precisely. 'I was just wondering how you'd feel if one of your operations got that kind of reception.'

'It happens.'

After she'd gone he tried to concentrate on his correspondence but his mind was full of sharp fragments from Mukesh's telephone call. He returned to the pathology report and scanned through it again. Maybe he could cram these cases into the rational scheme of things – breast cancer could get infected, so could a rectal tumour, and one end of a seminoma could outgrow its blood supply. But that was all small print, textbook stuff, and none of the cases fell accurately within the classical patterns. Kingsley chewed at the tip of his finger. The changes Mukesh described were freaks. They occurred rarely in isolation, far less in threes. On the other hand it was equally unlikely that a pathologist of Mukesh's seniority would make three such glaring errors in succession. Kingsley was not a betting man. When he was obliged to gamble with his patients' lives he did so on short odds and certainties. But suddenly the familiar laws of probability seemed no longer to apply.

Cranley, the mortuary assistant, had been across to Ranjits' Discount for his fags. To Cranley smoking was no longer a habit, but an integral part of his lifestyle. At home he had filled two drawers with coupons he would never cash, and made intricate working models with spent matches.

Now he was crossing Constitution Street, hurrying through a gap in the traffic with the peculiar swivelling gait imposed by his bad leg. The theatre porters had a joke about why he limped, but then the theatre porters had a lot of jokes. They had a joke about the dense black hair which grew from Williams's nose, a joke about where the ECG girl went at lunchtime, and a long and elaborate joke constructed around the picture-translation book for foreign sailors. Despite the sun Cranley still wore his black gaberdine buttoned to the neck. They had a joke about that too.

A ship's horn sounded from the docks as he crossed the car park, rounded the statue and entered the narrow close between anaesthetics and the mortuary. As he did so his body stiffened and a hot rush of blood suffused his face . . . The mortuary door was ajar and a man was coming out, an Indian, but of slighter build than Dr Mukesh.

'Get out of there,' he screamed as recognition dawned, and began a furious lolloping run up the close.

Dhangi looked up sharply then descended the steps, bringing the leather case with him. Cranley filled the narrow close, panting with exertion and fury.

'How the devil did you get in there . . . what the hell d'you think you're playing at?'

Dhangi was silent. He recognized immediately the futility of any explanation. He had been confronted by such people before, people so far from enlightenment that not even Shankara himself could have converted them. He was reminded of his brothers, Amrit and Bhopal, in the brick factory on the stinking Rishkamitri, of the psychiatrist in Amedabad, of Swami Vitthalnath's ignorant assassins – the *mlechcha*, the godless. Such a man was Cranley. Dhangi felt the righteous hatred curdle and congeal within him like *ghee*.

'What's in the bag?'

'Let me past.'

'What have you got there?'

Cranley made a snatch for the leather bag and caught one handle, but Dhangi's skeletal frame belied surprising strength. He tugged it away sharply, bringing Cranley's weight forwards on to his bad leg; then, seizing his advantage, he elbowed the older man viciously in the chest and forced his way past him.

Cranley thumped backwards against the stone. The corner of a buttress caught him in the small of the back. He lashed out wildly but his fist met with no resistance. Cranley straightened, grey and sweating, fighting for air. The stranger was already crossing the car park, eventually melting into Constitution Street.

Rather than attempt the steps to the mortuary, Cranley wrestled a cigarette from the package and placed it unsteadily between his lips.

He remained there, smoking and watching the railings long enough to make sure that Dhangi did not return.

*

34

Sheila had taken up cycling to school and back. Kingsley had opposed this to the point of buying her a new car but for once he didn't have reasons. She suspected it was just his good old sense of Edinburgh middle-class propriety.

She cycled past the bus queue. The schoolgirls with their berets crammed on their little heads shouted 'bye Mrs Kingsley', and she smiled at them. She had nothing to hurry home for. Alistair was rarely back from work before seven.

Autumn was the best season. Warm lemon sun and the coloured trees along Colinton Road. She would persuade Alistair to take time off. They could go to Denholm, take long walks, prune the roses, read, paint. Mr Oliver, English, tooted as he passed, craning discreetly over the sill of his Morris to look at her legs. She crested Church Hill. On a day such as this, across the valley of red roofs, one could see the Pentland Hills, and the artificial ski slope standing out like a thin white scar. She free-wheeled downhill, one leg straight on the pedal.

The paper usually arrived after they had both left the house. It was on the doormat when she entered. She took it through to the lounge, dropped it on the floor, switched the radio on, went to the bathroom and washed the school chalk off her hands. Then she went upstairs and put on her black leotard.

There was a square of bright sunlight in the centre of the lounge carpet. She closed her eyes, saw black and red, put her left ankle in her right groin and tried to empty her mind. After a while her leg started to hurt and she uncrossed it. The paper reflected the sun. Eventually it ceased to dazzle and she could read it: CHILDREN DIE IN M6 HORROR. She turned that page, leafed through idly. There was a small section on the woman's page: BREAST CANCER DIAGNOSIS – A CAUSE FOR CONCERN?

The article quoted the prevalence of the disease in Scotland. It went on to explain the diagnostic process of examining a frozen section of the lump for cancer: '. . . but how reliable is frozen section? Is every mastectomy really necessary? Recently the *Courier* has received information pertaining to one such

35

case – this mutilating operation performed on a young, active woman on the basis, according to the pathologist concerned, of "ambiguous pathology". The *Courier* investigates . . .'

Sheila Kingsley read this, scanned through it again, then licked her finger and carefully tore it out.

It was dark when Kingsley came home. He looked harassed. She kissed him. His lips puckered absently in return. 'What's cooking?'

'Casserole.'

He took off his coat and walked through to the lounge. He put his briefcase on the grand piano. Then she heard him opening a beer and imagined him standing with his back to the fire, toasting the seat of his trousers. He was quiet.

In the kitchen Sheila Kingsley took the newspaper article out of her pocket, crumpled it up and threw it in the bin with the potato peelings. She was surprised by a fat tear that ran down the end of her nose and dropped in the stew. She stirred it in. She didn't feel particularly sad but was aware of a vague foreboding which she could not yet identify.

5

The wind that dried the golf course had vanished now and the sky had turned a clear, remote blue. A breeze still loitered on the fairways. The city stretched below them like glasspaper, punctured by the castle and the blunt nose of Arthur's Seat – beyond that the Firth of Forth and the thin, grey coast of Fife. Richard Short wore slacks and the checked cardigan given him by his wife the year before their divorce.

There was no one before or behind them, only the cold distant birds and, somewhere over the rise, the phenomenally inefficient greenkeepers on loan from Gogarburn mental hospital.

'It's my belief,' Richard Short placed his feet carefully in the sand, 'that you should take a bloody great swipe with your first bunker shot. If you make contact you frighten the hell out of your opponent. If you cock it up you lull him into a false sense of security.'

Short raised his head to smile at his own glibness. His ball exploded from the sand, caught the lip of the bunker and sang off into the gorse.

'Nothing false about my sense of security,' said Kingsley. 'I'll help you find that.'

'Forget it, Alistair, I'll take another.'

'No harm in looking; those things don't grow on trees.'

'You certainly don't find them under bushes.'

'I do,' said Kingsley. He raked the ball out and tossed it back. Short's second attempt bounced twice and overshot.

Kingsley crouched on the green. 'I reckon you play your first bunker shot like every other shot – in isolation. Forget the psychological mumbo-jumbo, just play the shot. That's where people like Ballesteros win out.'

'That kind of attitude really gives me the pip.'

'It's called logic,' said Kingsley. His careful putt stopped just short of the hole.

Short glanced over at it. 'I'll give you that.' He chipped badly from the rough and put £4 on the debit side of his score card.

Kingsley filed his putter. 'Problem with you, Richard, is you never play the sensible shot.'

'Who needs sensible shots. You can destroy the game if you're too rational about it.'

'Can't be too rational – it's a rational world,' said Kingsley. He studied his finger. A gorse thorn had become imbedded deep in the tip. He pulled it out. Strangely the puncture did not bleed.

They played the next hole in relative silence. Eventually Kingsley said, 'Do you remember a patient called Sandra Spears?'

'No.'

'Yes you do. Pretty woman. I did her breast ten days ago.'

Richard Short looked blank. Kingsley continued. 'There was some artefact on frozen section. The husband phoned up and started regaling me with the fact that I'd operated irresponsibly.'

'Hope you told him to fuck off.'

'Not in so many words.'

'Cardinal mistake. I always tell them to fuck off.' Richard Short stooped to place his tee. 'Had a chap once, said my anaesthetic had rendered him impotent . . . silly idiot . . . oh, sorry, it's you to drive.'

'No, on you go.'

Short placed the ball and drew out a driver. His club came round in a long, lazy arc, then screeched downwards again, making contact with a satisfying crack. The ball lifted and swam off into the distance.

'You're driving's improved.'

'I've been practising a lot on my own.'

'Where?'

'At the hospital,' said Short.

'The hospital!'

'I've made a practice range – I'll show you later.'

Kingsley pictured Richard Short blasting away in the confines of the anaesthetic department. It seemed the anaesthetist's behaviour became increasingly bizarre with each succeeding year, as if he was trying to prove something.

'It's your birthday soon Richard, isn't it?'

'I don't have birthdays any more, Alistair. I just grow old disgracefully . . . Talking of which,' Richard Short lowered his club, 'how old's your secretary?'

'Rhona? She's thirty-four.'

'She's very attractive.'

'Yes?'

'Don't you think?'

'I don't know,' said Kingsley. 'She's my secretary.'

'Surprising she never got married,' said Short.

'Yes?'

'Don't you think?'

'Yes.'

'You're not listening to me.'

'No.' Kingsley was adjusting his grip and sighting on the green.

Short tucked his driver under one arm and swigged from his hip flask. 'Still thinking about the breast woman?'

Kingsley sliced his drive badly.

'I'm sorry,' said Short. 'I'm distracting you.'

Kingsley packed his driver. 'There've been others,' he said.

'Other what?'

'Like Sandra Spears – ambiguous pathology. Every patient I've operated on since. Chap called Niven with bowel cancer.

Then a seminoma, two prostates and another breast. Chandra Mukesh reports them all the same – "resolving carcinoma".'

Richard Short looked up quickly. 'No such thing.'

'Damn right.'

'Hell. He's not been misdiagnosing the biopsies has he?'

'I thought so at first. Gave him a bollocking. The bloody thing is he was right all along. The Royal confirmed everything he said . . . it's a totally undocumented appearance. Never seen before – cancer apparently melting away.'

'Christ – you could really be on to something.'

As they finished on the sixth green two figures appeared on the skyline behind them. Kingsley waved them forwards. He and Short moved over to the seventh tee waiting for them to play through. He took out his pipe and began to load it. Beneath them the grass fell away like the sweep of a breaking wave. Far in the distance the seventh green was the olive-yellow of iodine on skin. He cupped the match to his hand. The tobacco took light.

The cancer story had inflamed Richard Short's imagination. Now he was full of it.

'You see, either way you're on a real winner. Even if it is a total red herring, spontaneously resolving cancer is big news. The press will be on it like a shot.'

'The press *are* on it.'

'Well, fantastic. Just the kind of publicity we need. You can forget about them closing down the hospital. It certainly beats bloody gymkhanas and car stickers.'

Kingsley bit on the stem of his pipe. 'That's all beside the point, Richard. The fact remains. I've cut off a woman's breast, I've ripped out half a chap's bowel, I've ballsed up at least one old boy's waterworks. Now I'm told they might have recovered without the operation. Wouldn't that play on your conscience?'

Richard Short began to speak, then hesitated. Behind Kingsley the second pair had played out and were coming towards them: brisk, serious teenagers. It took them a few seconds each to place their tees, sight the green and drive. With the same long, serious expressions they replaced their clubs and strode off over the bluff.

'Has it occurred to you,' asked Short, watching them go, 'that you may have hit on some agent, something in the Leith atmosphere, I don't know – a mould, which kills cancer? Hmm? I know it sounds ridiculous, but have you thought of that?'

'No,' said Kingsley. 'I can't afford to think of that. It doesn't happen. And that's the kind of speculation I want to avoid. You know what would happen if someone started blethering about "cancer cures"? I'll tell you – total bedlam. Press all over the place. Clinics flooded with patients.'

'It's a great research project.'

'Nothing to research. It's all artefact.'

'Big news though.'

'The wrong kind of news. Fiction.'

'It's worth a fortune,' said Short.

'Not to me.'

Short placed his tee and sighed. There were times when Alistair Kingsley's principles were beyond comprehension.

Short was £1 ahead as they pitched towards the tenth. The sky was changing now, picking out the red from the rocks on either side, the gorse in comparison a violent yellow.

'Come on, Alistair, cheer up; there's going to be a rational explanation.'

'I'm glad you see that.'

Richard Short handed him the hip flask, already half empty. 'Maybe some joker tampering with the slides . . .'

'Can't be done . . . no way you could reproduce the detail.'

'I suppose you're right . . . or just some simple infective process. You know, like an abscess forming round Sandra Spears's breast lump.'

'Mukesh said it wasn't compatible with the histology. For

a while I thought maybe I was responsible. I thought maybe I was contaminating everyone I examined. Went to the length of washing my hands in Hibiscrub before each examination, sent a plate of my fingerprints off to bacteriology.'

'Nothing?'

'Nothing. How far d'you think?'

'Seventy yards?' Short flicked a cigarette butt towards the rocks. Above them the pink-bellied clouds converged westwards.

'Anyway,' said Kingsley, 'Mukesh has got other ideas.'

'What does he think?'

'Something allergic. He's been preparing slides for fluorescence studies.'

'Allergic to what?'

'God knows . . . the hospital? Me?'

Short was crouched, his back to the rocks, preparing to pitch. Now he laughed and called across, 'That's it, Alistair.'

'What's it?'

'You've acquired the healing touch.'

'Ingenious. And how do you account for that, Dr Short?'

'I don't know. God moves in mysterious ways. Maybe you were good when you were little.'

Kingsley guffawed. Short smiled. His pitch landed three feet from the flag.

The light was failing as they left the clubhouse and climbed into Richard Short's silver car. The city was reduced to a spreading black stain between the hills and the estuary.

'Are you sober enough to drive, Richard?'

'Drive? I'm sober enough to fly.'

'Don't demonstrate.'

'Drinks at the Royal Forth,' said Short, 'and on the way there I'll show you my practice range.'

'What practice range?'

'My golf practice range – at the hospital.'

'Let's go straight to the club.'

'It won't take a minute.'

'If you insist,' said Kingsley.

He buckled his seat belt and the car revved away.

What was it that had worried him about the hospital these past few mornings? Driving to work, the old place now filled him with a strange apprehension. In the evenings he left with a sense of release. Kingsley moved uncomfortably in the bucket seat. Fifteen years he had worked in the Douglas Calder. It had its faults, but Kingsley had had a great affection for the old place. Now it was somehow different – violated.

They locked the car. Beside the main door the hospital's air vents snored like sleeping alcoholics.

Richard Short led him through the corridors, childlike in his excitement. They called into his room in the anaesthetic department. Behind the door of his office Short kept an old driver. In the bottom drawer of his desk a lump of putty and a bag of old golf balls. 'You'll love this, you'll love this,' he kept saying, chuckling his obscene throaty chuckle.

They passed McCallum and Barton wards on the second floor. Richard Short led him out through the fire escape. A blast of warmth followed them from the hospital, then the cold harbour air, sobering, refreshing. The iron railings were caked with rust.

'You're sure this is quite safe, Richard?' It was the voice of responsibility. Kingsley quelled it. Perhaps the same sentiment as he had felt all those years back as he and Roderick McDonald fastened their undergarments to the flagpole at the City hospital; the old spectre of propriety which he found so impossible to shake off – dispelled then by the precedent of undergraduate foolhardiness, now by alcohol and curiosity. Nothing changed. He envied Short's lack of self-consciousness – there was true sincerity.

They were on the roof now. For a moment Kingsley lost sight of his guide. Then, as his vision adjusted, he discerned the nimble grey shadow stepping over pipes and vents, picking a route between the opalescent skylights. Kingsley followed less confidently. He caught up with Short at the northern edge of the roof. Below him the harbour water looked solid as coal. The street lights on the bridge duplicated themselves in its surface and a matt, forgiving blackness obscured the slums and warehouses. By night Leith was almost beautiful.

'Are you coming?'

Kingsley looked round. 'Where are you?'

'Down here, there's a ladder at your feet.'

His toes found the rungs. He climbed down. They were standing in a narrow well, two yards wide by three yards long, open at one end, facing towards the harbour and lit by two caged bulbs. Short walked towards the open end and placed the lump of putty at his feet, then he fished in his pocket for a golf ball and pressed it on to the putty. He handed Kingsley the club.

'You drive, Alistair.'

'Where?'

'Out there of course, into the harbour.'

'You must be joking. What about the offices?'

'Here,' Short took the club back. 'Nothing to worry about, they're all empty. Nobody does anything in there anyway. Unless you totally duff it, it's not going to drop on the road, and the bridge is five hundred yards away at least.' He stood, legs astride, loosening his shoulders. 'You just make sure you don't hook it to the left, towards the tenements. You've got to make a really poor shot to miss the . . . *Whack* . . . the water.'

The ball rushed into the night. Short waited, shoulders hunched in apprehension. Nothing.

'Not sure that I go along with this, Richard.' Kingsley took the club.

'Minimal risk, Alistair, minimal.'

'Besides,' he said as Kingsley lined up to drive, 'we save the buggers' lives every day. This kind of thing evens up the balance. Whether you like it or not you're one of fortune's executives. Aim for the crane – see the light. It you hit anyone he's hellish unlucky. Had it coming anyway . . . keep to the right now. Straight into the harbour and you're safe as . . .

The wood whistled. A sharp click, the ball vanished into the night.

'. . . as houses,' said Richard Short.

6

The body of an old woman was laid out on the slab. It had been in the fridge for two days now and the surface had turned a glossy yellow. The incision, clean through skin, muscle and bone, began at the apex of the chin and ran to the centre of the pubis. Heart and lungs were still in place, congested purple against the pale flesh. The abdomen was an empty pit. Cranley had removed the abdominal viscera and was now twisting the neck of a plastic sack that contained them. He sealed it with wire and took it through to the anteroom. He held up the bag.

'You'll have finished with her?'

Chandra Mukesh looked up from the dictaphone. He looked at the bag full of guts and pulled at his chin, momentarily confused by Cranley's free use of the personal pronoun. Then he said, 'No, hang on, Mr Cranley, I want a bit of that vertebra. I'll be finished with this in two minutes.'

He offered up an apologetic smile which Cranley devoured in a clattering of false teeth and a smouldering soliloquy in which the words 'Hangin' about all day' featured prominently. Mukesh returned to his dictation. After two months working with Cranley he was slowly learning to accept the old man's choleric demeanour as the normal, against which less perceptible mood swings might be judged. All this week Cranley had been slightly more irascible than usual.

Mukesh, on the other hand, was feeling quite pleased with himself. The weight of academic opinion had swung behind his interpretation of the aberrant pathology slides. He would soon be given the opportunity to present his findings at the Royal Infirmary. Following that there was always the chance of a small research project. Mukesh had come a long way since leaving India. His intellectual prowess was complemented by a keen yearning for success and now the smell of possible advancement was wafting under his delicately flared nostrils.

In the mortuary he tied on an apron and handed Cranley the chisel. 'I am not very skilled at this, Mr Cranley. Perhaps you will do me the honours.'

This gambit was calculated to mollify the old mortuary assistant. It was a matter of some pride to Cranley that he could still outshine most young pathologists at the more arcane aspects of morbid carpentry. He took out the chisel, sucking contemplatively on his dentures. Cranley was suddenly communicative.

'The trick is,' he placed the chisel on the diseased lumbar vertebra, 'to not go too low. It's a matter of the angle of the whatsisname isn't it. Put it like this,' Cranley indicated an acute angle of the chisel on the bone, 'you're knackered, aren't you?'

Mukesh nodded encouragingly.

'You go straight through the spine,' Cranley explained. '. . . Now put it like that,' he lowered the handle of the chisel, 'and you're away.'

By way of an explanation he delivered a sharp tap to the handle of the chisel, knocking off a neat sliver of bone. Mukesh caught it in the specimen pot.

'Cancer,' said Cranley knowledgeably.

'Yes, a secondary from the ovaries.'

'That's one that didn't work,' said Cranley.

Mukesh continued to study his section. A dense pale area indicated where tumour had invaded the spongier bone.

'What did not work?' He took the formalin from the shelf, tucked the great brown flagon under one arm and covered the specimen.

'Yon thingummy.' Cranley was threading a needle. 'Kingsley's new treatment.'

Mukesh looked up sharply from the specimen pot. 'What new treatment?'

'The cancer cure,' said Cranley. 'So William says.'

Chandra Mukesh scratched his head. In his short stay at the Douglas Calder he had already learnt the truly seminal role of William Galbraith, head porter, in hospital gossip.

'I am afraid he has misinterpreted something there,' he ventured.

'Is that a fact?' Cranley had threaded his needle. Now he placed the bag of guts back in the abdominal cavity.

'We've just had some unusual pathology results. There's no question of a cancer cure.'

'Is that a fact?'

Cranley began to sew, taking big bites on either side of the incision and pulling the thick cord tight. His lips corrugated with effort as he pulled.

'I hope you'll tell Mr Galbraith.'

'Aye, I'll tell him.'

Cranley's free hand crammed the bag of guts under the advancing stitches. 'It's what I thought.'

'Good.'

'Ye can't cure cancer,' he observed, pulling at another knot. 'Wouldn't be right. Cancer's God's work – like fishes.'

Dr Mukesh did not attempt to untangle this parable. He was satisfied that Cranley had the basic message. That kind of rumour could do a lot of damage.

Mukesh returned to the anteroom and resumed his dictation. Halfway through he stopped again. A thought had struck him. Cranley was hosing down the mortuary floor. He turned off the hose as Mukesh entered. A thin trickle of water fell on the blood at his feet, making small, pink ferns on the tiles.

'William, the porter,' said Mukesh. 'He knows what goes on in the hospital.'

'That's his job,' said Cranley defensively.

'Maybe I should let him know I have seen a rather strange fellow hanging around here recently – an Indian chap.'

'That bastard,' said Cranley with a degree of venom which took Mukesh off guard. 'Is he a friend of yours?'

'Good gracious me, no. I just wondered if the security should be informed of him.'

'They've never been any help to me,' said Cranley acidly.

'In what way was he bothering you?'

Cranley sucked at his false teeth and breathed through his nose. The very presence within hospital bounds of a tramp like Dhangi inflamed him to a degree which he could not explain. 'Shouldn't be here,' he said gruffly. 'Got no business has he? Caught him out the back messing about with flower petals and suchlike, singing songs or whatever.'

'Yes,' said Mukesh. 'He had the appearance of a holy man.'

'Holy? You call that holy?' Cranley exploded. 'The man's off his head. Damn near assaulted me the last time I saw him.'

'When was that?'

'Just recent. Caught him half in and half out of this place. Asked him what he was doing and he thumped me. He's no more holy than fly in the air.'

Never before having exchanged more than a few sentences with the older man, Mukesh felt a new sense of concord with Cranley. He leant back against the dissecting table and inspected the punctured toe of one boot. 'Perhaps you're right,' he conceded, 'but then again it's a funny thing the Hindu religion. You wouldn't believe what these fellows get up to. In my country they are all over the place – begging for food, starving themselves, this thing and that thing. And some of the beliefs! My God! Do you know it's quite common for some of them to drink cow's urine, or smear themselves with dung. The ancients, the Aghoris, believed you could not communicate with God unless you practised cannibalism. It's quite fantastic, no?'

Alerted by the sound of running water, Mukesh looked up. Cranley had lost interest some time back and had turned on the hose again.

'Anyway,' Mukesh shouted, 'I agree – this fellow was most unpleasant.'

Cranley continued to ignore him.

'Incredible thing is he said he was a doctor ... I suppose it could be true,' Mukesh reflected. 'He was asking some questions about the pathology business which were quite technical ... But then he threatened me! Asked me to give up my job and leave the hospital! Can you believe it?'

Deaf to all this and mildly exasperated by Mukesh's failure to recognize the end of the conversation, Cranley turned the water pressure down. 'What's that you're saying?'

'Nothing important,' Mukesh said. 'The Indian chap. He wanted to work here.'

'If he does,' Cranley returned, 'it'll be over my dead body.'

Mukesh naturally assumed he was joking.

At about the same time, Alistair Kingsley received a telephone call in theatre. It came at the end of a heavy list, just a further irritation, along with the dropped instruments and the poor lighting, on an afternoon that had already strained his patience to breaking.

'Someone answer that,' he growled, as he laboured away in the dark, bloody hole. The patient was an immensely fat woman in her mid-forties. She had complained of symptoms for several years, and now, when they came to operate, the gall bladder was a blighted little organ, welded to the undersurface of her liver.

Kingsley clipped at the surrounding tissues, up to his forearms in fat.

'It's for you, Mr Kingsley.'

Kingsley said nothing.

'Mr Kingsley's not available,' said the nurse on his left.

Kingsley cut further and was met by a brisk jet of blood. He cursed.

'Clip.' He applied, with difficulty, a small metal clip to the bleeding point. 'No light,' he added tersely. The anaesthetist had not relaxed the patient sufficiently and retraction was impossible.

At this point a voice behind Kingsley said, 'He says it's urgent.'

'Who says it's urgent?'

'The phone call, sir.'

'Ask him if it's a matter of life and death.' Again the footsteps retreated, the swing doors whump-whumped, then the footsteps returned.

'He says yes.'

'Damn and hell.' The clip had slipped. Kingsley fried the vessel with cautery and tore off his gloves.

'Carry on, Steve.'

In the corridor his hand on the receiver was slippery with sweat.

'Yes?'

'Mr Kingsley?'

'Who is this?' Kingsley demanded.

'It is Dr Dhangi.'

'Dr who?'

'Dr Dhangi,' said the nervous voice, '. . . we met in the hospital car park, yes?'

Kingsley tore furiously at the cloth ties of his gown.

'Yes, I remember you, Dr Dhangi,' he said. 'Look. I don't know what you think you're playing at but you've dragged me away in the middle of a very tricky piece of surgery. If it's about a job, I'll tell you now . . .'

'It is not simply about a job.'

'Well perhaps you'd like to tell me what it is about.'

'We must talk . . . ,' Dhangi said, anxiety filleting his speech,

'. . . you are having certain problems . . . I think I can explain . . . this thing is very important.'

'What problems? What do you know about it?'

'There is much to discuss . . . I must see you.'

'See me about what, for God's sake?'

'There is a public house near here . . . the Carriage Bar? . . . I will be there tonight . . . six o'clock.'

'Listen,' said Kingsley. 'If you want to meet me, whoever you are, you can damn well phone my secretary and arrange an appointment. I'm not going to see you in some bloody dockland dive . . .'

He was cut short by a rapid succession of bleeps from the call-box. The noise stopped briefly and he heard Dhangi saying with renewed urgency, 'Six o'clock . . . six o'clock . . . you must . . .' Then Dhangi in turn was interrupted, this time by the mocking rattle of the dead line.

Kingsley smeared a hand over his forehead and returned to theatre. He stood over Steve Jennings's shoulder.

'Problems, sir?'

'No.'

Jennings had opened the duct to the gall bladder. Now he was carefully feeding a catheter into the opening. He secured it in place, drew back bile, and injected contrast medium. 'Ready for X-ray.'

Kingsley glanced at the clock on the theatre wall. Four thirty. If the bile duct was clear they'd be finished by five. Forty minutes to check the wards and finish up at the office. Ten to reach the Carriage Bar.

He had already been round McCallum ward with Sister Taylor when the rest of the team arrived. There were no major decisions to be made on the male wards. Kingsley jostled them round with the sister whipping files out from the trolley like hot toast and the houseman scribbling furiously on drug charts.

He left Barton ward till last. It always took longest.

'We're in a bit of a rush, Sister McReady.'

McReady barred his path, hands on hips. 'Leslie Cairns wants to know about her breast lump.'

'I know,' said Kingsley, failing to sidle past.

'Dr Jennings said it was malignant.' She fixed Steve Jennings with an accusing stare, then looked back to Kingsley.

'Provisionally that's right,' he said.

'Mrs Cairns doesn't know that,' McReady persisted. 'I told her seeing she's not scheduled for a mastectomy she could assume it was OK.'

Kingsley grunted in agreement. 'That's right, isn't it?'

'Yes, sister . . . well, no.'

She turned on him. From the utility room there came a clattering of bed-pans and the flushing of the sluice. Down the ward, his patients had already set about the cosmetic adjustment of bed-linen which signalled they were aware of his presence.

'Why are we doing all these routine cases,' Sister McReady wanted to know, 'all these hernias and gall bladders?'

'They're on the waiting lists.'

A nurse passed. McReady stopped her and adjusted the girl's hat. 'But you've had a couple of mastectomies waiting for the past week . . . and the woman with the sarcoma.'

'Yes, I'm trying to avoid cancer surgery for the meanwhile. We're having a few problems with the specimens.'

'There's been a lot of anxious ladies on the phone wondering about the stoppages. It's worrying for them, you know.'

'It's worrying for me, sister. We'll get it sorted out.'

McReady hung in like a newshound. 'How long d'you think it's going to go on for?'

'Oh, a couple more days.'

'What are you going to tell Leslie Cairns about her breast?'

Kingsley scanned the faces in the wards. Half hidden behind the nursing station he could see Leslie Cairns in a floral nightie, pretending to read. 'I'm not going to tell her anything just now. I'm in a bit of a hurry . . . ,' he said. But when they reached her bed his sense of duty got the better of him.

It was a quarter to six when he got to his office. Rhona was wearing a pair of tight black trousers, and a beige tunic, belted at the waist.

'You're still here?'

'I'm waiting for a lift.'

She took out a small bottle, tapped some perfume on to her index finger and dabbed it behind her ears.

Kingsley walked through to his office. There were two more lengthy pathology reports on his desk. Rhona came through.

'There was a journalist on the phone today.'

'What did he want?'

'He was doing something for the *Courier*. I don't know.'

'Roland Spears. It'll be about his wife.'

'That's the one,' said Rhona, writing it down.

'Tell him I'm presenting her case at the Royal. He's welcome to come if he wants.'

'Are you? – Is he?'

'Yes,' said Kingsley.

'If he rings again I'll tell him,' said Rhona, then she looked over his head, through the window. 'Here's my lift. 'Bye.'

The vestiges of her perfume hung over Kingsley's desk as he packed his briefcase. He checked his watch – ten to six – and pulled on his coat.

The car park was half empty. Kingsley threw his briefcase in the side door and locked it. His collar was uncomfortable and a sensation not unlike hunger was dragging at his stomach. Near the gate he noticed his secretary stepping neatly into Richard Short's idling Porsche.

Constitution Street was turgid with evening traffic, bumper to bumper, engines choking. The bus queue stretched the length of the Co-op. Kingsley turned away, down the side of the Douglas Calder, past the scrawled gang slogans on Causeway Lane. He walked past the wrestling hall, a poster on the wooden ticket booth: 'DR DEATH, THE MASKED MEDIC — LEARN THE SCIENCE OF PAIN'. A sheet of newspaper blew around Kingsley's ankles as he passed the social security. Crossing the road he joined the stream of traffic now nosing over the harbour bridge. Kingsley kept pace with it. At the traffic lights he crossed the road again, past the burnt out slums and the old port authority. He could see the Carriage Bar from here. One small bright fire, like a baker's oven, in the black tenement block. For the first time he faltered, then, pushing both hands into his pockets, he crossed the cobbles and hurried towards it.

7

Inside the Carriage Bar the single low, dark room was crammed with drinkers. Kingsley squeezed inside. Dockhands were three deep at the bar, those in front greedily downing pints, those behind waving pound notes in some obscure benediction over their heads. Above them a line of plastic hops had grown a tacky skin of cigarette tar. The same brown film covered the once white walls and wrestling posters. There was no sign of Dhangi.

Kingsley moved towards the bar. A man burrowed out from in front of him and the crush of humanity sucked Kingsley in, shoving and shouldering him on his way. Someone pushed away from the counter and Kingsley fought his way into the gap. He called his order several times before the barmaid consented to pour him a whisky. The drink sloshed onto his hand. Kingsley paid her and pushed back into the body of the pub. The press of workmen closed in on the gap he had left.

There was a lot of activity round the podium to his right. Kingsley scanned past it, wrestling this way and that to get a clear view of the tables at the back of the room. Something told him that Dhangi had already arrived – a physical sensation of the man's presence that was so far removed from anything he had previously experienced that Kingsley would never have acknowledged it. But sure enough, in a far corner, he eventually spotted the ragged Indian.

Kingsley elbowed his way towards the corner, pushing occupied chairs forwards in order to squeeze between them, grunting apologies to their occupants. Dhangi seemed completely oblivious of his approach. As Kingsley drew nearer he noticed that Dhangi's eyes were closed and his breathing slow and regular. One hand rested on the table, index finger and thumb touching lightly across the palm, as if encircling the stem of a glass. Kingsley stopped just short of Dhangi's table. Dhangi made no sign of acknowledgement, nor did he respond to his name. Kingsley turned to leave.

'Mr Kingsley.'

Dhangi's eyes were suddenly wide as if he had been wakened from a deep sleep. Kingsley felt irritated and insulted by the gambit. He remained standing. 'Look I've had second thoughts, Dr . . . Dr Dhangi. I can't see this meeting is going to be of much value to either of us.'

'No, you are wrong . . . sit, please.'

'I mean if you think you're going to impress me with gamesmanship . . .'

'I have no games.'

'. . . I've honestly got no idea why I came here.'

'Stay . . . I beg you.' Kingsley pulled a chair back and consulted his watch. 'I'll give you five minutes.'

'This may take some time.'

'Better get on with it then.'

Dhangi fidgeted with the sleeve of his shirt. From somewhere to Kingsley's right the blare of a jukebox rose above the hubbub. Kingsley glanced sideways to see a girl in a black nylon négligée mount the podium. The dockers aggregated round her, jostling for position.

'I cannot tell you how long I have looked forward to this meeting,' Dhangi began.

'Don't.'

'You must understand . . . it is difficult for me to explain . . . we have such different backgrounds.'

'You told me you were medically trained.' Kingsley made no attempt to hide his scepticism.

'That is correct.' Dhangi continued to pull at a thread on his cuff. 'I studied in Jalore . . . my family were very poor . . . I was awarded a scholarship on account of my school grades . . . they had high hopes for me . . . but other things have developed since then.'

'You didn't qualify?'

'Oh yes, I am qualified . . . it is not about medicine I wished to speak . . . it is about the other thing.'

'What other thing?'

Dhangi's eyes raked Kingsley's face, as if seeking some fingerhold on its stony surface. 'Do you believe in God, Mr Kingsley?'

'Look, I honestly don't have time for a philosophical debate. If you've got something to say, say it.'

'I'm sorry . . . I'm sorry . . . do not be distressed.' Dhangi held his hands up in supplication. 'Here,' he followed quickly, 'I will show you something.' He reached into his inside pocket. Kingsley half expected him to produce the wad of references he had presented at their last meeting but instead Dhangi brought out a battered leather wallet. His fingers rummaged through its contents and lighted on a folded slip of paper. 'Please study this.'

The paper was yellow with age and fragile from repeated folding. Dhangi opened it carefully to reveal a faded print with a heading in Hindi script. He smoothed it flat with his palms and passed it across the table where Kingsley regarded it with less than passing interest. It was an old photographic reproduction of a rock-carving, apparently ripped from a book. The rock-carving depicted a building of some sort. The lower corner of the page had trailed in a patch of beer. Kingsley was distracted by a roar from the vicinity of the podium as the stripper divested herself of her stockings.

'Do you recognize it?' Dhangi was asking.

'No.'

'The hospital . . . no?'

Kingsley looked at the picture again. The relief did bear an uncanny resemblance to the back of the Douglas Calder – steps leading from the water, a broad, cobbled forecourt, four storeys of high, arched windows flanked on either side by two squat minarets corresponding to the hospital's twin towers. There was even, at the bottom left-hand corner, a cubic outbuilding where one would expect to see the mortuary. He looked up. Dhangi did not smile, but his eyes bored into Kingsley like gimlets.

Kingsley was nonplussed. 'Interesting. Where did it come from?'

'The picture is from a book of archaeology . . . the carving can be found on the wall of a shrine in the Arravali mountains in Rajastan . . . However, the building it depicts exists only in myth. In Hindi it is called Nigambodh Ghat – the River Temple.'

'Nonsense. Let me see that picture again.'

Once more Dhangi passed the paper across the table. Kingsley spread it out and scrutinized it, managing for a few moments to forget the increasingly stifling atmosphere of the bar, and the vaguely fungal smell of Dhangi's clothes, immune even to the girl on the podium, now being exhorted to unclip her bra.

'Can I keep this?' he asked.

Dhangi shook his head. 'I am afraid that is not possible.'

'Can I take a copy of it?'

'I would be unhappy about that also,' said Dhangi spiriting the picture back inside his jacket.

Kingsley shrugged. He felt it was time to confront the real issue. 'Well then,' he said, 'as an expert in illusion, perhaps you'll tell me how you've been interfering with my work.'

'I was coming to that.'

'Let's stop beating about the bush. You're a doctor, right? You've just shown me you have some skill at forgery. I know for a fact you've been snooping round the pathology labs where Dr Mukesh fixes our slides. Now is it or is it not unreasonable to assume that the problems we've been having with certain specimens are in some way your doing?'

'It is not unreasonable,' Dhangi conceded.

Prevarication infuriated Kingsley at the best of times. 'Oh, for God's sake,' he shouted. Conversation stopped at the adjacent tables. Heads turned towards them.

Dhangi quickly turned his face to the wall. 'Please,' he implored. 'This is not simple . . . it will take some time.'

'That's what I don't have.'

'You see,' Dhangi continued, 'as a medical man you cannot be expected to believe what I am telling you . . . I would have felt the same once . . . perhaps I should tell you my own story.'

'I'm sure it's unnecessary.'

'It will help, I promise.'

Kingsley sighed and ran a finger under his collar then leant back and folded his arms. Dhangi took this as his cue. Where to begin? He closed his eyes and saw his village by dawn – a shambles of mud, dung and corrugated iron on the banks of the corrupted river, the yellow dogs and piles of smoking garbage. A young man – himself, Acharya Dhangi – was picking his way up the mud track at the start of his daily journey to medical school. 'I was a diligent student,' he began. 'I studied medicine day and night for five years. I won several prizes. My family were very anxious for me to succeed. Often my brothers said, "Why should this one be given money for clothes? All he does is read his books while we are working, working to support the family." But my mother encouraged me. If I had become a city doctor their problems would be over . . . however, it was not to be. Just before my final exams I began to suffer from nervous symptoms – depression and other things. I became severely ill . . . next thing I remember was the psychiatric hospital in Amedabad . . .'

Dhangi faltered. The mention of psychiatric illness obviously confirmed Kingsley's preconceptions about him. So what of the rest? Perhaps he should not tell Kingsley of the mystical inner voice which had beckoned him to Varanasi, of his flight from the hospital, or of those tormented, chaotic days which followed, wandering from town to town, village to village, without even a few paise to buy his fare on a bullock cart. Kingsley was looking pointedly at his watch. Panicking, Dhangi hacked through the confused, tangled memories and arrived at a stained mud doorstep in Varanasi.

'. . . The man who effected my recovery was not a doctor, he was a holy man, a Swami . . . I met him in Varanasi.'

Varanasi. Yes, Dhangi could still see the vast flights of steps to the water, the endless funeral processions, the temples decked with sculpture and draped in pigeon dung, the air full of tattered flags, of scavenger birds and of the smell of the dead.

'I was drawn to his house. I was very ill from malaria and roundworm. But he recognized me immediately from our past lives together. I believe he had sent for me. He took me in and I stayed with him till I was strong enough to return to Jalore and continue my studies. But Swami Vitthalnath had opened my eyes you see. I was pledged to devote my life to Lord Krishna . . .'

Dhangi hesitated again. Kingsley was still as far from comprehension as Dhangi's mother was that afternoon by the water tank. He could remember her slapping her *saris* on the flat stones, and he recalled with painful acuity her expression when he told her he was renouncing everything she had worked and suffered and prayed for all the twenty-seven years of his life. His hands shook as he took the folded betel leaf from his pocket and placed it in his mouth. He held the wad in his cheek, swallowed the acid saliva and continued.

'. . . I returned to Varanasi and lived for another five years with Swami Vitthalnath – a true holy man, a great man . . . he knew the Vedas entirely . . . our scriptures, every verse he knew by memory. Every day we spent in prayer and medita-tion . . .' Dhangi's voice softened as he recalled the guru – one eye dulled from trachoma and his torso scarred from neck to waist from the austerities he inflicted on himself. '. . . He knew,' Dhangi whispered. 'Yes . . . he alone knew the truth of the Hindu faith . . . the essential truth, that rebirth can only be achieved through decay . . . you see . . . it is so simple. We are surrounded by it – rotting and decay. Even here this harbour is rotting. In India it seems the whole country is rotting. You see! . . . the Gods provide the means and we ignore them. We build our houses from cowdung but cannot recognize the very bricks from which to rebuild Vrindaban on the banks of the Jumna!'

There was a pause. Kingsley shook his head coldly. 'I'm sorry,' he said, 'I really don't understand where all this is taking us.'

'I don't ask you to understand. I performed the *pujas* for five years and did not understand. I spoke with God without understanding! And the crowd who murdered Swami Vitthalnath did not understand. How could they? They had no knowledge, could not see the purpose of these practices. So, they dragged him down the steps to the river and beat him to death with sticks. How could I make them to understand, I who had no understanding!' Dhangi's inflamed eyes filled with tears and he covered his face convulsively with one hand.

Kingsley had long experience of distancing himself from other people's emotions. He watched dispassionately as the Indian wiped his eyes, then blew his nose between finger and thumb. 'I'm sorry,' Danghi resumed, 'I found him two hours later, you see, dead . . . lying by the water . . . the kites had already taken his eyes . . . but he had left a message in the sand . . . a reference to a certain verse in the *shruti* . . . it was there that I found myself.'

Dhangi grasped Kingsley's sleeve. A fierce light appeared behind his tears. 'I mean this truly. I *found* myself. A reference to myself. In the Atharvaveda – the oldest literature known to man. A collection of prehistoric hymns and chants, half of them beyond any sensible interpretation. I am in that book. As you are.'

'What am I doing?' Kingsley asked dryly.

'In the Atharvaveda it is written that a healer would cross the black waters in search of Nigambodh Ghat, there to perform the prescribed rituals . . . imparting to a man of the *pandava* – a palefaced one – the power to heal by touch, to the eternal glory of both our people and the salvation of the godless . . . so be it.'

Dhangi checked himself, as if on the brink of some obscure litany. The stripper, naked now, was running her hands over her gyrating hips. Kingsley prised Dhangi's fingers from his arm. It was time to leave. 'A palefaced one,' he repeated.

'A British person,' said Dhangi, 'like yourself.'

'Like myself, eh? And how is he described?'

'He will be a man of infertile seed, born with a sixth finger on his right hand.'

It struck Kingsley that Dhangi was certainly adept at his job. The fine scar on the edge of Kingsley's fifth finger was almost invisible, but Dhangi could have noticed it when they shook hands before in the car park. Again, to an unscrupulous member of the profession, hospital records were no secret. 'You claim to be a doctor,' he said.

'Oh yes.'

'You've worked in other hospitals round here.'

'Briefly . . . in Glasgow.'

So that was it then. Dhangi had some background on him, he'd found out about the business with the pathology slides, had done a bit of checking up off his own bat and was using the combination of established facts and gleaned information to perpetrate some kind of pseudo-mystical con. Kingsley rose stiffly to his feet as the music stopped, suddenly acutely aware of the choking atmosphere and the passage of time. He would have to catch Sheila at the theatre. God only knew how he'd allowed this bedraggled stranger to take up so much of his evening. 'I'm sorry,' he said to Dhangi. 'I'm not convinced.'

'But it is written,' Dhangi was desperate, 'it is written, it is the Word,' he said, 'the Word which is first-born mother of the Vedas . . .'

'So you say,' said Kingsley. He tried to move away but Dhangi's bony hand was hanging onto the hem of his jacket. 'For God's sake,' said Kingsley, 'what do you want from me?'

'Give me a job in the mortuary. That is enough. There I will perform the necessary *pujas*. I will be your priest and you will become an *avatar*, an embodiment of God.'

Kingsley was finally convinced. Con-man or not, Dhangi was definitely mad. 'Let me go,' he bellowed.

The men at adjoining tables fell silent again, anticipating a fight.

'Listen here,' Kingsley lowered his voice. 'I wouldn't dream of employing you even if I could. We already have a pathologist – a Dr Mukesh. There's no vacancy.'

Dhangi spat on the floor, his saliva was stained crimson with betel juice. 'That *candal*. You are contaminated by his shadow. You have no need of him.'

Kingsley wrenched himself free. 'Well, I certainly have no need of you.'

'You will,' said Dhangi. 'Here, take this.'

But Kingsley did not stop to examine what Dhangi had pressed into his hand. He was already pushing past, shoving Dhangi and his chair to one side then barging through the close-packed chairs and tables towards the bar. Momentarily disorientated, he looked around for the door then flailed towards it like a tired swimmer, sweeping men from his path, fighting through the thick broth of sweat and tobacco smoke. At the door he turned. Dhangi had followed him part of the way; now, stranded, he shouted something over the hubbub but only the silent movements of his betel-stained mouth reached Kingsley who, turning, pushed outside. The door swung to behind him and he breathed deeply. Only then did he look at what Dhangi had given him, a scrap of brown paper on which there was scrawled, in pencil, an Edinburgh address. Kingsley tore it in quarter, then tore it again and scattered it into the night. Then he set out towards the bridge. Over the water the hospital glowed in the twilight, like the candle-bedecked façade of Nigambodh Ghat.

Rhona caught the ball against her heaving chest. Now her serve arched high over Richard Short's racket and into the back corner. Short flicked it out against the side wall. She ran forwards and caught it before the bounce, smashing it back to the opposite corner. Richard Short thundered across the back of the court and missed it completely.

'Nine all,' he said, breathing heavily. She had tied her hair back in a pony tail and her legs were glossy with perspiration. He returned her next serve with a scorching low smash which she couldn't return. 'I'm sorry. Very ungentlemanly.'

'I'm not sure gentlemen play squash with ladies in the first place.'

They swapped sides. Richard Short once more resisting the impulse to reach out and squeeze her bottom *en passant*.

'These shorts are a perfect fit.'

'Don't be crude.' She glanced up at the gallery to check that no one had overheard.

'I'm surprised you never got married, Rhona.'

She served an ace. 'Ten–nine, Richard.'

'I wasn't ready,' he complained.

'That was my problem too,' said Rhona ' – just keeping you on your toes.' She crossed court again and won the last point easily.

Richard Short wasn't concentrating.

'Actually there was a chap once,' she said as she retrieved

her cardigan from the far corner, 'but in the end he wasn't my type.'

Short held the door open for her. 'What was wrong with him?'

Rhona dropped her shoulder and slipped through. 'No style,' she said, 'all hands.'

'Know what you mean. See you in the foyer.'

Sheila Kingsley sat in her beige coat, one hand draped over the arm of the sofa. Her black hair was a dense mane of newly formed curls; a tear drop diamond earring hung from either ear. She rang the hospital again. They confirmed that Alistair had left half an hour previously. She checked her watch, stood up, inspected herself in the mirror. Underneath the coat she wore her dark blue gown. She toyed with the diamond at her neck – she had overdressed on purpose – then she dialled for a taxi. He'd probably dropped in at the Royal on business. She had come to accept the health service's continual poaching on their marriage.

The curtain had just risen when Kingsley sidled along to the empty seat. He sat down. Her hand sought the reassuring fold of fat above his waistline.

'Where have you been,' she whispered, 'laying the secretary?'

'No,' said Kingsley, 'laying a ghost.' He sat down, straightening the creases of his trousers, and focused on the performance.

Sheila sniffed his jacket. 'You've been in a bar.'

'I'll tell you later.' Her arm sneaked through his and he relaxed into the upholstery.

At first he was glad of the dark. He looked down at his hands in the semi-darkness, cracked his knuckles. Then the anger subsided and he could allow himself to be absorbed by the fictional horrors on stage . . . 'Discomfort swells, mark King of Scotland, mark.'

At the interval he bought her a gin, remembered to compliment her on her hair and made an excuse for his lateness. Dhangi's crazy meandering vanished from his mind. The chandelier of the theatre bar scintillated like the bright, idle chatter round them and Kingsley, normally scathing about the trivial sham of Sheila's theatrical friends, felt elevated, purged, restored.

The meeting with Dhangi had taken him no further forward. But in some ways, Kingsley reflected, it had given him valuable insight into his own present state of mind. It amazed him now that he had ever linked this Dhangi character with the more complex worry about the pathology results. He was obviously getting that whole issue out of proportion, festooning and obscuring it with smaller, trivial anxieties. He looked forward now to presenting the cases at the forthcoming clinical meeting. It was obviously high time they were assessed more objectively.

8

Like a bear in a pit, Kingsley paced the floor of the steep wooden amphitheatre, concentrating on his feet. For the third time he checked the remote control for the slide projector. He attended these meetings every week, but normally declined to present the material. It smacked of showmanship and, quite apart from his natural shyness, Kingsley disapproved of showmen. Working where he did, Sheila had accused him of reclusiveness. But for all their squalor, Leith docks still fostered the anonymous toil which had paid for the Douglas Calder.

These meetings took place in the Infirmary, slap in the middle of town – a vast rambling mausoleum with all the furniture of the new medicine in the architecture of the old. And if Kingsley remained apart from it he knew its citizens: white-haired fathers of the profession, uncombed medical registrars, groomed young surgeons and knots of students with loose-leaf binders.

They filed in slowly at a rate determined by the women serving coffee. As the lecture theatre filled, Kingsley continued to pace his semi-circular confine. He carried a pointer and occasionally he tapped this lightly on the floorboards. Since his meeting with Dr Dhangi the previous week there had been no further sign of the dishevelled Indian around the hospital. And, happily, over the past week the ambiguous pathology results had ceased to relay back from Chandra Mukesh. The previous cases remained a mystery. Kingsley planned now to expose these to scientific inquiry. There remained a niggling doubt that he was somehow playing along with a drunken vagrant's joke.

Richard Short edged into his seat. He polished his glasses and adjusted the distance by which his Van Heusen cuffs emerged from the Jaeger suit. He was here out of loyalty. He rarely attended these meetings, the intellectual atmosphere being usually too rarefied for his tastes. Now he looked around for someone to talk to. He was sitting next to a man he didn't recognize, a thick-set young man with vibrant red hair who was sucking a pen and studying the assembled audience with a critical, if not hostile eye.

'I don't think we've met?'

'I don't think we have,' said Roland Spears.

'Richard Short,' said Short, extending his hand.

'Hello,' said Spears, shaking it.

'What do you do here?'

'I don't do anything here.'

'What do you do then?'

'I'm a journalist.'

'I see,' he persevered. 'What brings you to a medical meeting?'

Spears turned again. 'I'm interested in one of Mr Kingsley's cases.'

'Anyone in particular?'

'My wife,' said Spears. His expression discouraged further inquiry. Short gave up and turned to speak to someone else. Then the lights went off.

There was a whirring of a small fan as a projector came on, then the single thick shaft of light. Kingsley shielded his eyes and stepped to one side. He addressed himself to the stacked, silent darkness.

The slides came up and Kingsley began to talk, at first rather more quickly than he had intended. Then, gradually, his awareness of the audience melted. They became a coughing, rustling wall to his dark confessional. His speech was a catharsis. He told them about Sandra Spears, the pretty young woman whose breast he had removed. He admitted that the other operations had not been straightforward. One of the prostates was having difficulty with urinary continence and Niven's colostomy was tending to prolapse.

'Side effects which are acceptable only if the operations were absolutely necessary.'

Richard Short looked downwards on Kingsley, a lone figure by the light of the projector. Beside him the journalist was scribbling noisily. Kingsley looked upwards into the crowd.

'With this in mind I'd like you to judge the following pathology specimens for me. It's a surgeon's nightmare,' he said. 'I just don't know what to make of them.'

Mukesh came forward. Kingsley handed him the pointer. In the penumbra he smiled at the younger man. They had made their peace; he had apologized to Mukesh for his initial insults. But the damage was already done. There was no real remedy for the loss of respect between them.

The first pathology slide came up, painting Mukesh's white coat with the whorled pink and purple designs of the tissue sections. Mukesh's presentation was lucid and rehearsed. He explained the malignant features evident in the cells, then pointed out the anomalies, the apparent halt to invasion, the areas of necrosis, of encapsulation.

'The pathology suggests, impossible as it is, that had we not operated, these cancers might eventually have resolved . . .'

The 'we' was a gesture of professionalism and generosity. Another uncomfortable truth: he had totally misjudged Chandra Mukesh.

Kingsley took the lectern again for the discussion period. The lights came up in the auditorium as he asked for comments. By convention the first pronouncement belonged to the professor of pathology. Knowing this, the professor allowed a few moments to pass before he hoisted himself to his feet. He had white hair and small pink eyes, a red button of a nose and far below, in the centre of the acreage of cheeks and chin, a small pink mouth. He spoke with a high breathy voice of which most students could manage some form of imitation.

'Most interesting cases, Alistair, most interesting, and I'm sure we all fully appreciate the delicacy of your recent decisions.'

He dabbed with a finger at one eye. 'I for one would entirely endorse the diagnoses – these slides show cancer.'

At the lectern Kingsley fought to suppress a great smile of relief. Beside Short, Spears stopped writing.

The professor continued '. . . but there *has* been some kind of reaction. The features are allergic. Can we have the last slide – yes, fine – now there you see cancer cells as Dr Mukesh so rightly pointed out. I can't understand the profusion of eosinophils – these white cells here.' The shadow of his pudgy finger appeared in the projector beam, obscuring the critical portion of the picture.

'But there you have it. As I say, I would favour an allergic explanation.' He stroked his white hair. 'But God knows what allergen would elicit a parallel reaction in such different forms of tumour.'

With that the professor sat down. Kingsley opened his mouth to speak but his words were pre-empted by a buzz of excited conversation. The professor, however flamboyant, was not noted for his flights of wild conjecture. But what he had suggested was totally unprecedented.

The chaos showed no signs of abating. Kingsley rapped on the lectern for order.

'You're suggesting,' he said, 'that over a short period certain cancer sufferers in Leith may somehow have been immunized against their disease.' It was the rather sensationalist explanation that Short had proposed during their golf match, and Kingsley was surprised that the professor espoused it so readily.

'Exactly,' he announced, 'identify the causative agent

71

and . . . my word . . . this could be an accidental discovery of colossal importance. Rivalling penicillin – greater.'

The lecture hall erupted once more and the professor sank back in his seat with a small smile of satisfaction. Gradually Kingsley, as chairman, took some control over the controversy. From the boiling auditorium explanations and suggestions were thrown up and exploded with the speed and violence of a clay pigeon shoot.

But Kingsley was happy simply now to have placed himself behind the firing line. It was agreed he had operated on cancer. As for the present discussion, Mukesh would get a research project out of it, but Kingsley doubted his investigations would prove fruitful. He had watched this kind of speculative enthusiasm burn itself out on more than one occasion. After the initial flurry of interest, a paper here and there, a series of letters to the *B.M.J.* The initial findings would accumulate critical re-appraisal, like weed around a propeller till finally they drifted back into the mainstream of scientific thought. His universe was in order. Until Henley spoke.

Henley was a neurology registrar. He had remained silent for the duration of the meeting, sitting five rows back with his arms folded across his chest.

Now, parting his white coat, he rose to his feet and wedged two fingers into the lower pockets of his waistcoat. Henley dressed, spoke and practised medicine with the elegant precision of a prosecuting counsel.

'I must say,' he began, 'a lot of the more esoteric immunology which has been bandied about goes quite above my head.'

Laughter. As the golden boy of his generation Henley could afford this kind of self-deprecation. 'I wonder if we could all look at the fourth slide. There are a few features that most people seem to have missed.'

The projectionist located the slide. It appeared on the screen. It was a plain photo of the cancerous testicle.

'I'm intrigued,' said Henley, 'by the distribution of the

necrotic areas of this tumour. These strange oval markings —
like . . . like fingerprints . . .'

Kingsley wheeled on the projector screen. Henley was right!
Looking at it now, what had at first seemed to be random
areas of inflammation actually corresponded to a pattern of
overlapping fingerprints. Worse, they were clustered at the
lower pole of the tumour – the area accessible to examination.

'And the sixth slide,' said Henley.

The same. With the eye of faith, distinct 'fingerprints' at the
lower pole.

For most of his audience, the simile was not an emotive
one. 'Fingerprinting' was, as Henley was quick to point out,
simply an imperfect description of the patchy inflammatory
response observed, for example, in ischaemic colitis. But
Kingsley, eyes still transfixed to the screen, found little
reassurance in this. From somewhere in his memory there
came the chilling echo of Dhangi's voice, through the brown
flux of cigarette smoke and darkness in the Carriage Bar – the
healing touch?

'Another thing,' Henley continued relentlessly, 'is that most
of these cancers resolve asymmetrically. Starting superficially,
the curative process proceeds inwards. Something has come
in contact with these tumours inducing a local, not a general-
ized, response.'

Henley swept back his perfectly pressed white coat and
lowered his hands to his trouser pockets.

Kingsley's neck prickled. He shot, in the half-light, a guilt-
stricken glance round the auditorium, but they were not
looking at him. They were looking behind him at the screen.
In the rapt silence Henley spoke again.

'A third observation: we have seen cancers at several stages
of resolution. The first breast lump was just beginning to
resolve. The second cancer exhibited very few remaining
cancerous cells . . . whatever the curative agent, if the rate of
response is constant, it must have been applied to the

malignancies at different intervals before operation . . .' Henley paused '. . . I don't have any explanations for this, but I throw in the observations for what they're worth. Arguably they only serve to obscure the whole issue.'

But in Kingsley's mind it had all become transparent and delicate as ice. Yes, he had examined Sandra Spears two days before her operation. The subsequent breast cancer patient he had examined ten days before operating. The others took their places in that spectrum, their degree of resolution proportionate to the interval between his touch and the eventual operation. The healing touch? It was absurd, impossible, he could not believe it . . . or *would* not?

The light came up. More offers from the floor. Kingsley steadied himself on the lectern, appeared to listen, but his thoughts were in rout. Memories swarmed over him now, like flies to a wound, seemingly validating Dhangi's ridiculous claim – the strange warmth he had experienced on feeling the cancers. Mrs Stoke, the other breast woman, had jumped and complained of the heat of his fingers. The heat? Niven felt 'ten times stronger, doc.' the day after his examination. The fantastic made sense.

Now the meeting was over. Those on the higher tiers filed out on the galleries to either side. Most of the men near the front were his peers, the senior consultants. As they left via the door at the front of the lecture hall, behind the lectern, Kingsley cast his eyes down, taking great pains over the shuffling and filing of his notes.

'Very interesting.'

He looked up to find Cullen, the orthopaedic surgeon, offering a huge palm.

'You all right?'

'Yes, fine thank you, Tony.'

A traffic jam formed behind Tony Cullen and he moved on, surprised by Kingsley's untypical vacancy.

The others filed before him, smiling and nodding. Sometimes a word. Kingsley said little. They passed by him and out into the bright, clattering corridor. Kingsley, shocked and expressionless, avoided their eyes like a man in an identification parade. Eventually, finding a handful of colleagues around him, he managed to chat about the possible course of Mukesh's research. The topic afforded him some consolation and he found himself warming to the subject. Moments ago he would have been prepared to bet that research on the cases would ultimately prove fruitless. But now he was forced to pin his hopes on it. That or nothing. What Dhangi had suggested was beyond science.

9

Kingsley glanced across at his wife. She appeared to be watching the scenery. He was still occasionally caught off guard by her beauty. His eyes returned to the road. She moved across and put her head on his shoulder.

'Do you love me?' he asked.

She sat up again. The question was spectacularly untypical.

'Why do you want to know?'

'Just wondered.'

'Of course I do,' she said, settling herself. Kingsley leant back, relishing the rolling, fluid motion of the car. The town had exhausted itself, petering out now in tentacles of roadside cottages.

'Why?'

'Why what?'

'Why do you love me?' said Kingsley.

'What are you getting at?'

'I'm not getting at anything. Come here. I just want you to tell me.'

'Well, you're never usually interested. It's a bit worrying, out of the blue like this. You're not building up to tell me something?'

He smiled.

'All right then,' she said at length, itemizing the points on her fingers.

'You're sincere, and honest . . . and straightforward . . . and principled . . . and fantastically conventional . . .' she broke off. 'God, I don't know, Alistair, you never asked me before. Why do you want to know?'

'Just looking for reassurance.'

They drove on in silence.

'What do you need reassurance for?'

Kingsley shrugged. 'Nothing. Just every now and then things start gnawing at your self-confidence.'

'You're still worried about that cancer research thing.'

Kingsley winced. She had an uncanny knack for identifying his problems. 'What do you know about that?'

'Just what you tell me. Which isn't much. You don't approve of it?'

'It's nothing to do with me,' said Kingsley.

Nothing to do with me. He was gradually persuading himself to believe that. He cast his mind back to his meeting of the day before:

Mukesh was perched on a high stool in the window of the pathology lab. when Kingsley had entered. He turned from the tube-racks and bottles of stain.

'Sorry, Chandra, don't let me disturb you.' Kingsley helped himself to a stool. Mukesh followed his lead and sat down again. 'I just dropped in to see if you needed any help getting this research project on the go.' Kingsley leafed through a stack of files on an adjacent table. 'You're obviously not wasting any time.'

Mukesh smiled modestly. 'I am just acquainting myself with the patients a bit more fully. It's quite possible they all had something in common before they arrived here.'

'Absolutely.'

Mukesh pointed to a sheaf of papers with the pipette he was holding. 'At the minute I'm drawing up a draft question-naire asking them all about their past medical history and so forth. The oustanding common factor is, of course, that they all came with cancer during the same two weeks. So I need to look at everyone who came with other complaints during that period, and at those people who presented with cancers at the same time but elsewhere.' Mukesh indicated the staining work he had in hand and shrugged. 'I'll find time for it all somehow.'

Kingsley patted him on the shoulder. 'We can cut out a lot of the repetitive paperwork with the computer,' he said, 'and I'll see about finding you a research assistant.'

'That would be most kind of you, Mr Kingsley.' Mukesh seemed genuinely encouraged.

Kingsley fingered the fine control of the microtome. 'The fact is,' he admitted, 'I still feel rather guilty about having cast aspersions on your initial observations.'

Mukesh's walnut skin darkened to a rich mahogany. 'It's of no importance, Mr Kingsley. As a child in India I became accustomed to insults. My mother's family were Untouchables.'

'I know,' said Kingsley, then hurriedly corrected himself. 'I know about that kind of thing . . . I mean I was talking about it recently . . . I met a Hindu man who was full of that kind of nonsense.'

'You saw him too?' Mukesh's dark brows rose. 'That Brahmin – that holy man? You talked to him?'

'He collared me and blethered away,' Kingsley said evasively. 'Said he was a doctor, wanted a job blessing the hospital or something – I don't know. You don't believe that sort of mumbo-jumbo do you, Chandra?'

'I'm a Hindu,' said Mukesh, 'but only in name.'

'This holy man seemed to take it all pretty seriously.'

'Oh they do,' said Chandra Mukesh, 'but in India there are almost as many holy men as there are cows. It follows that most of them are terrible charlatans.'

Kingsley had agreed wholeheartedly and walked back through the hospital with the feeling of having significantly reinforced his stance against superstition.

Now he flexed his hands on the steering wheel – normal hands, he told himself, the hands of an artisan.

The car climbed through the valley to Dalkeith, a pile of pointed, grey houses on the ridge above. Half a dozen idle teenagers were loitering round the shopping centre. Sheila chose this moment to drop her next bomb.

'Who's Roland Spears?'

One wheel caught the edge of the experimental roundabout. The car lurched, then Kingsley turned southwards towards the Borders.

'He's a journalist.'

'I know. There was a newspaper article.'

'He apologized to me for that. He was mad about me removing his wife's breast. In the end I think he gathered we can't cure cancer.'

'You never know. Your Dr Mukesh might make a big break-through.'

Kingsley patted her thigh. Personally he didn't believe in breakthroughs. He saw medical science as a great ponderous dredger advancing inch by inch, sifting and distilling. Every now and then it came up with a nugget. But the process itself was the important thing. Being a part of that had its own rewards.

'Things don't change that fast.'

'Well, you have,' she said.

'In what way?'

'You normally don't put your arm round me when you're driving.'

The sun was setting as they reached the Gala water, nudging and flirting with the road, wide sweeps of water behind the fir trees. Nervous sheep crammed the grass verges as they passed and the car dug into the darkening landscape, rolling itself in a rich quilt of heather, grass and bracken.

They called in at the caretaker's cottage and picked up the keys. Jackie stood framed in the door of his cottage with the dogs in his shadow, the little Yale key in his huge red hand.

He talked about the dipping. Up at the cottage Kingsley put on a pair of gloves and brought in the coal. The night, punctuated by the rasping of his shovel, was full of noises – distant crying sheep, the creaking of the Scots pines, a pair of quick soft wings, the almost inaudible sucking and crackling of his pipe.

Inside Sheila was winding all the clocks. Kingsley turned on Radio 3 and life seeped back into the room. Beige walls; pink sofa; the thinning Persian rug; iron latches on every door. Upstairs a lonely wind rattled the loose window.

They cooked dinner together. The smell of dust was displaced by the smell of the fire, then, in the kitchen, a mixture of garlic and pipe smoke. Then they sat elbow to elbow on adjacent corners of the heavy oak table, saying little. When Kingsley chewed, a muscle on his temple corded and relaxed. She pressed it with a finger. Something classical and embalming played on the Bakelite radio. They ate, shared silences, exchanged smiles.

While she bathed he was flicking through an Agatha Christie. He didn't usually read detective novels, but the book shelf offered few alternatives – Mrs Beeton's Cookery Book, The History of Salt, Across Africa by Land (printed in 1910) and What Katy Did.

By the time she came out of her bath he had lost interest in reading and stretched out from the sofa with his feet on the hearth.

'What are you thinking?'

'Just thinking.'

'Hospital stuff? You're not indispensable, you know!'

'I agree.'

'You don't usually.'

'It's easier to see things in perspective now . . . down here.'

She sat on the sofa with the towel wrapped like a turban on the top of her head and licked his nose. The log fire farted and whistled. His hand was warm on her stomach. It rested there, curled and heavy like a sleeping dog. Later it moved upwards, smoothing her skin, nudging the soft underbelly of her breast. The bath robe had fallen open. Firelight played on her breast, leaping and dancing on the plump contour. The nipple sprang between his fingers.

'Do you feel anything when I do that?'

'Yes,' she said, beginning to unbutton his shirt.

'No, I mean anything abnormal . . . warmth.'

'Yes, warmth,' she said luxuriously, then kissed him.

The old bed was piled high with quilts and blankets. The varnish had aged on the paintings, reduced in the moonlight to polished black squares. Sheila kicked off her slippers.

'Why are you laughing?'

'Slippers – my mother used to call them passion killers.'

'They don't work.' Kingsley encircled her waist.

He rarely spoke when he made love, sometimes groaning as his mind thickened with lust, sometimes a sigh of release at the moment of orgasm. Sheila would whisper incessantly, hum, coo, blow in his ear. Beyond her soft coaxing gibberish he could hear the clanking of the grandfather clock and the various complaints of the stolid old bed. Then she said *Ah!* very loud and straightened both legs.

'What.'

'Cramp. Ah, hell. Get off.'

Kingsley fumbled among the books and glasses for the switch of the bedside light. When it came on, her face was contorted with pain.

'Where does it hurt?'

'My leg. This one. Oh. Ah.'

He began to rub at the muscle. 'You never usually get cramp.'

'Well, I've bloody got it now. Oh, hell. God!'

Kingsley kneaded and mashed at the flesh. Sheila's string of expletives devolved to a staccato of agony, bordering on tears.

When the pain subsided, the bed was in turmoil. Quilts and pillows littered the floor. Kingsley started to laugh.

'It's not funny.'

He smacked her bare bottom.

'What causes it?'

'Yoga and cycling.'

'Rubbish. What can I do about it?'

Kingsley closed his teeth on the bundles of muscle at the back of her neck.

'Roll over,' he said, 'and I'll show you.'

In the deep impenetrable sleep that followed, Kingsley had a dream: two images in succession – the first was of Dhangi, his dark face suspended in the Carriage Bar. Kingsley was watching him from a distance, from the far door. The cigarette smoke cleared, and there was Dhangi's face, looking at him, as he had looked at him before, manic and accusing. The red mouth moved and Dhangi's reedy voice came clearly across the void between them, as if from a separate person by his side. He turned, pushed through the door, to be confronted not by the docks, but by Henley, and behind him the banked, wooden amphitheatre of the Infirmary lecture hall. He strained to recognize the faces that filled the auditorium. Colleagues? Inquisitors? Then he searched Henley's clear, bright expression. Henley was waiting for something. They were all waiting for something. His confession. He opened his mouth to speak. Then Henley dissolved and faded, the listeners faded, the tiered wooden seats melted into nothing and he was looking at a window – the small wooden window of the cottage bedroom, and beyond that the black Denholm countryside.

Kingsley lay back and tried to sleep.

He awoke to butter-yellow sun pouring through the window. There was a crescent of cobwebs at the bottom of the lower pane. He walked through to the bathroom and produced a rattling, bellowing symphony from the ancient plumbing.

He splashed water on his face and searched unsuccessfully for his sweater, then padded through to the kitchen. He cooked bacon and eggs in an iron frying pan, drinking milk from the jug and skating lard around the circumference of the pan. He cracked the eggs, fabulously undamaged, and shovelled thick slabs of bread under the grill.

Sheila was painting in the garden. He wrestled with the latch and the window swung open.

'Have you eaten?'

'I'll have a coffee,' she said.

'What are you painting?'

She turned the canvas towards him.

'Very good.'

She made some reply he couldn't hear. She was holding the brush between her teeth. She took it out. 'How did you sleep?'

'OK.'

'You were thrashing about a lot,' she told him.

'What, before or after?'

When she laughed a small puff of condensation appeared in front of her mouth. Kingsley turned back into the kitchen. The toast was burning.

When he came back to the window she was engrossed in her painting. Kingsley surveyed the garden. Jackie had cut the grass but the vegetable patch was burgeoning with cabbages and the roses needed pruning. Sheila was facing towards the hill, painting the copse of Scots pines at the foot of the garden. Beyond, Sickle Hill rose in a long, gentle plane of brown and purple, then blue sky, traversed by idle clouds. A small bird stirruped across the lawn. The toast was burning again.

After lunch they climbed the hill, the valley stretching below them like a complex green tartan. They could see the river from here, and the small castellated turret of Lord Moncrief's folly. Jackie was rounding up sheep in the corner field: at times his distant whistle pierced the wind. Sheila turned.

'Why didn't you tell me about Spears?'

'Because I was worried and confused . . . I didn't understand what was happening. You wouldn't have been able to help. It would just have made you miserable too.'

'It did make me miserable. I thought we were heading for a divorce. Besides, how do you mean I wouldn't have been able to help you? Sure, I don't understand medicine, and all the technical stuff, like pathology, but I do understand guilt.'

'I didn't feel guilty.'

'Yes you did, you looked like Martin Borman. It was all to do with Spears, wasn't it?'

'Yes,' he told her.

'I'm just hurt you didn't share it with me.'

'I'm sorry.'

'Accepted,' she said.

'Coming on?'

'No – I think I'll go back. My leg's beginning to hurt again.'

He crouched down in the heather. 'Where does it hurt – here?'

'No, a bit higher, just above the knee,' she said.

'Does it hurt when you move the knee itself?'

'No. It's just a dull, sickly pain. It comes on when I put weight on it for a long time, or sit in certain positions.'

'What about when you move your hip?'

'What's that got to do with it?'

'Well, it could be referred pain,' he told her.

'What's that?'

'Well, it means what's wrong isn't actually where you think it is. You identify the pain as coming from one place, the knee, but it's actually being caused more centrally, in the hip. It's due to the nerve connections.'

She prodded him. 'You're so wise, Alistair.'

They began down the hill again. The heather forced them to take long steps. By the time they reached the pond, Sheila was limping noticeably. Back in the cottage Kingsley got her to take her trousers off and lie on the bed. He felt the painful spot. Nothing. Then he bent her knees up. Then he sat on her foot and rocked her foreleg backwards and forwards. There was no pain. Then he examined her hips, pressing in the groin over the head of each femur, crossing and spreading her legs as far as possible. He bent her knee and rotated the foreleg like the hand of a clock. The hip rotated perfectly in its socket. Kingsley slipped unconsciously into his professional tone of voice – the virgin uncle. 'Maybe you've got a bit of arthritis. We'll get Tony Cullen to X-ray it.'

Sheila Kingsley folded her long brown legs. 'There's just one other thing, Mr Kingsley, before you go.'

'Isn't this called professional misconduct?' he asked as she pulled him towards her.

'No,' she replied. 'It's called physiotherapy.'

Kingsley climbed over the ridge, through the long dense wood that crested it, like a cockscomb, and down to the small, grey, chiming village. The trees on this side of the ridge were mainly deciduous, following the line of the path, their trunks tangled in hedgerow and undergrowth. Beyond Denholm the river wound on in a glistening silver band towards Hawick.

Mrs Strachan had become like her store – colourful, untidy and all-providing. 'Well, Mr Kingsley. We've not seen much of you these weekends.'

'I'm keeping busy.'

'I thought you must be having an epidemic.'

She lingered over the first and middle syllables, throwing the word into relief. Kingsley smiled. He told her what he needed. She knew the tins like a librarian. Then he bought some fishing flies – a Black Spider, a Bloody Butcher and a Greenwell's Glory.

As Sheila made tea he sat at the table and made a cast of them, the Butcher on the end of the main strand of nylon, the other two on droppers. Later, at dusk, he assembled his rod and set off across the fields. The cows followed him, inquisitive, mournful lowing shapes in the twilight. Kingsley sat on the river bank and cast upstream. It was a difficult cast. In the light a line fouled in the trees was more or less irretrievable. On the other hand, this pool looked as though it had fish in it. The river took a sharp turn here. The water had gouged into the red clay, deeply undercutting the far bank. His cast dropped well upwater. He saw the nylon line glinting on the surface, then gradually sink along its length as it swept around the corner.

He performed twenty, thirty such casts, the line chirping above his head, the cast landing on the fast stretch above the pool and drifting past him. Then it came – a sharp tug. He countered by raising the point of the rod and he was into something. His line tightened and fled downstream. Over the sound of the water came the swift rasp of his reel. He allowed the fish a bit of line, then wound in as it gave him slack. It was swimming upstream now, or lying low under the bank. Kingsley waded in up to his knees. Then it was off downstream again. He applied firmer pressure, allowed the fish to tire itself out, then, reeling in, coaxed it into shallower water. It was hardly fighting now, coming towards him in slow zigzags. Kingsley waded in and netted it. It was a big one, probably a cannibal, almost two pounds. On the shore he dug into the net and brought it out, its body arching sideways in rapid muscular spasms, its mouth wide. With the hand which held it Kingsley could feel an unfamiliar irregularity of the body. Holding it up to the light he perceived a ragged line of rough nodular structures running from the ventral fin on one side and extending under its belly. The fish was diseased. Kingsley put two fingers into its serrated mouth and twisted the hook out, pulling against the barb. Then he placed the trout back in the water and it sank out of sight.

10

Anthony Cullen was a big man. He filled the chair awkwardly, like a lump of granite in a digger. He came from Glasgow but these origins were only part responsible for the timbre of his voice, significantly altered by twenty years of short, fat cigars. When he spoke there emerged from the depths of his dark suit a noise not unlike the growl of a bear.

'If it isn't the lovely Mrs Kingsley.' He extended a huge hand and she placed her own within it.

'Have yourself a seat. I've had a wee word with Alistair — you've been having pains in your leg.'

'Well, actually,' she demurred, 'I've hardly noticed them these past two weeks.'

'Amazing what a spot of country air'll do for you. You thought it was the knee joint?'

'Well, I did originally. Then I thought it was a bit higher. I can bend my leg quite painlessly.' She demonstrated.

'Excellent — you'd get a job as a Tiller Girl; just get behind there and whip your tights off. What's happening with the famous research project?'

'Nothing much. Alistair's letting his pathologist get on with it. He's more or less washed his hands of it himself.'

'I don't blame him. I've never understood the fascination of peering down a microscope all day. Spend all your life hunched up contemplating things no one can see — it's like being in church. Are you ready back there?'

'Yes,' she called. She heard his chair push backwards. Then he swept aside the screens and inspected her.

'You never had arthritis in the past?'

'No.'

'And your family are all free of it?'

'Yes, as far as I know.'

'OK. Alistair couldn't find anything on examination?'

'No.'

Meanwhile, like a plumber bending a pipe, he put her through the movements Kingsley had performed.

'Fine pair of legs,' he pronounced. 'In perfect working order. We'll get you an X-ray. I don't think there's anything wrong there at all.'

She took the slip he gave her and the nurse directed her down to X-ray. She waited fifteen minutes before they called her in, then lay on the couch as a girl manipulated the heavy machine above her. After a while the technician gave her the films in an envelope and she returned to wait outside Tony Cullen's consulting room. The waiting room had filled now. The man in front had one arm supported at right angles to his body on a complex plaster gantry. Of the five people in her row two had their arms in slings, one had his leg in plaster and a third, when she glanced again, had no foot. She felt fraudulent, sitting amongst them with no obvious stigmata of disease. Cullen, ushering the previous patient to the door, called her in immediately, ahead of the others; double fraud.

'Right,' he said, taking the films from the cardboard envelope. 'Let's have a look at the snaps.' He slotted them into the viewing screen. An iridescent glow illuminated their faces.

'That's your lower leg. See that? Tibia. Fibula. Down there, is the top of your ankle joint. Nothing wrong there. Do you want to keep them?'

'No thanks.'

'Fine, fine.'

The next film was her hip and femur. When he looked at it, Tony Cullen stopped saying fine.

He took it off the plastic clips and held it up to the window.

'All OK?' she asked brightly.

Initially he didn't answer her. He squinted obliquely at the film in his hand, then returned it to the screen. He raised a big hand and stroked slowly at the lower half of his face. Then he cleared his throat. He took a pen from his top pocket and indicated a lobulated, clear area in the upper part of her femur. 'You see this, Sheila — that's . . . not absolutely normal.'

'No?'

'I think we want to look at that a bit closer.'

'What do you think it is?'

Tony Cullen looked at her directly. He exhaled from an imaginary cigar. 'First of all I'd like to give you a more thorough examination.' He switched off the viewing screen almost with exasperation, like a late night horror film in which he had lost interest. 'At this stage it's difficult to say.'

She studied his big face. She didn't mention cancer. Everybody had that kind of nightmare. If she said cancer he would roar with laughter and tell her to put the thought out of her head. He'd pat her benevolently and tell her not to be ridiculous. Cancer was like shark attacks, horrible but infrequent.

'What sort of thing are you thinking of?'

'Well . . . ,' said Cullen.

'Could it be cancer?'

'. . . Yes.'

In the silence that followed she bit her lip and took a couple of deep breaths, trying hard to keep her eyes wide open. She formed a few words of reply but no sound came into them.

Tony Cullen put a great branch of an arm over her shoulder.

'It's one possibility of many, but it's a possibility that you should be aware of. It's doubts and suspicion which really wind people up. I know Alistair feels the same. Once I've re-examined you I'll take some blood tests. We'll need to arrange for another picture — a scan. Maybe we'll eventually have to bring you in to take a sample of the bone. Are you all right now?' His handkerchief was the size of a napkin. 'Do you want me to explain things to Alistair?'

She tidied her hair with one hand.

'No . . . No, I'll tell him myself first.'

She looked around foolishly for somewhere to put the handkerchief.

'Here,' said Cullen, 'I'll take that. Give us a wee smile. Whatever it is we're sure to be able to do something about it . . . one way or another.'

'It was a disaster.'

'What's the problem?'

'Oh, its just awful.'

'Looks all right to me.'

'Well, I suppose there's nothing I can do about it – except the chop.'

'I'd just let it grow.'

Rhona pulled at her fringe. 'Well, I suppose I've got to live with it.'

Richard Short continued to study her with his mouth full and a look in his eye which suggested that he was capable of devouring something more substantial than the ice-cream in front of him. At the moment his attention seemed to be focused on her neck. Unconsciously, she covered it with one hand.

'. . . and I wish you wouldn't look at me like that.'

'Like what?'

'Like you were planning to rip all my clothes off and cover me in treacle.'

'There's an idea.'

She smiled. 'Will you get me a coffee?'

'Is that what they're calling it?'

Richard Short rose from the table and walked over to practise his charm on the ladies who served behind the canteen. He had originally opposed the plan to merge dining areas for medical and non-medical staff. But the arrangement had its advantages. It certainly made it easier to bump into Rhona pretty regularly without appearing over attentive.

He walked back with the coffees. Rhona appeared to take a long and rather encouraging look at his crotch. As he sat down again she asked, 'What have you got in your pocket?'

'Ah – those? – golf balls . . . old golf balls.'

He seemed eager to expand on this subject but Rhona denied him the pleasure. She had a pretty astute idea now of Richard Short's intentions towards her. There was a fair chance that she might ultimately allow him some success. In the meantime he was childishly eager to impress and it was possible to derive a fair bit of amusement at his expense. So rather than let him tell her what he did at the hospital with a pocketful of used golf balls, she smiled, adjusted her blouse, pushed back a strand of hair and inquired no further. Their feet met under the table. She moved hers away an inch or so.

'How about dinner tonight?' said Richard Short.

'That's very kind of you, Richard, but I really don't want to go out in public until I get used to my new hair.'

'I wasn't talking about eating in public.'

'Are you a good cook?'

'Is the Pope Catholic?'

She gave a little smile, half suppressed by pursing her lips. The net result was a kind of pout.

'Are you going to attempt to seduce me?'

'Would you object?'

'I'm not sure.'

'It would help your hair curl.'

'I can always use a heated roller,' she said.

Rising to her feet she leant lightly on his arm with just enough of a smile to make Richard Short suspect that she had intended the *double entendre*.

He watched her bottom disappear through the polished wooden doorway. When the serving lady came to take his plate away he was sitting back in his chair with the air of a poker player who has been dealt what he thinks is a winning hand.

Sheila Kingsley was curled on the sofa, mentally constructing the coming conversation with her husband – ' "Have a good day, Alistair?" "Yes, fine." "Have a whisky?" "Thanks, what are we celebrating?" "Not celebrating, I'm preparing you . . ." "Don't tell me you've smashed the car." "No . . . I saw Tony Cullen." "Oh yes?" "He says . . . he says . . ." '

Pull yourself together, Sheila. She folded her legs on the sofa and tucked the shirt in to her skirt. ' "Alistair." "Yup." "Guess what?" "Don't know." "Sit down, this is going to be a shock. I've probably got bone cancer." '

No, she'd leave it till after dinner. She pulled the skirt over her knees and closed her eyes. She had exhausted her fury and despair walking back through town until her leg ached, buying a blue and white dress she neither liked nor needed.

In their bedroom the new dress lay unopened on the bed. Outside, beyond the foot of their garden, a wind was blowing through the hermitage. The mature trees broke and gathered like the sea. She had wandered through the guest rooms, through Alistair's study with its leather-topped desk and rows and stacks of medical journals. Back through the lounge, the dining room and into the conservatory, even down into the basement to inspect the stack of logs and the rows of home-made wine. She had ended in the upstairs bathroom, crying into the sink. She had cried herself dry and felt much better. She went down to the kitchen, poured a gin, put on Vivaldi and curled up here on the sofa. She had left the television on with the sound down . . . Now she could sleep for days.

When she opened her eyes there was a picture of an Arab with a rifle. It had grown darker outside.

Alistair's car on the gravel.

The front door opening.

His call.

'Hello,' said Kingsley.

'Hello,' she said. '. . . Kiss.'

He stooped to kiss her.

'What did Tony say then?'

She took a sip of gin, swallowed it too fast and choked.

'Oh, he doesn't know – there was something on X-ray.'

'What sort of something?'

'Oh, you know, a medical sort of thing. A lesion.'

Kingsley sat on the sofa. His arm came round her, tightened, like a rope round a climber's waist, and she let go, dripping her mascara on his grey and white striped collar.

Alone in the hall, Kingsley phoned Tony Cullen's house. It rang twice, then Cullen picked the receiver up.

'Alistair, I was waiting for you to ring. She asked straight off and I had to tell her.'

'What did you find?'

'Well, she's probably told you as much as I can. It was the last thing I expected. I thought the X-rays might show a bit of erosion just. But there's something worrying just below the greater trochanter. It's not a bone cyst.'

He stopped, allowing Kingsley to draw his own conclusions.

'The thing is, Alistair, reviewing the X-rays, I wouldn't be surprised if this is a primary tumour of bone.'

'It's not very common at her age is it?'

'Don't see many of them. But it's what I'd put my money on.'

Kingsley pinched his forehead. He was trying to remember the first time she had complained of pain. She'd joked about getting old and stiff driving to Paris in July. Who could tell how long the thing had been growing in her leg? 'She tells me you've booked her for a bone scan.'

'Yes, tomorrow or the next day.'

'Then?'

'Well, there's no point messing about. I think we'd want to get her straight in for biopsy. Maybe next week. I've also booked a whole body scan. That'll show us straight off if there's a metastic tumour anywhere else.'

Kingsley laughed dryly.

'Why do you laugh?'

'The whole body scanner – I've always regarded it as an expensive research tool.'

'Well, I'm sorry if it's against your principles.'

'God no, I'm getting used to discovering my own hypocrisies.'

'Happens to all of us as we get on.'

There was a pause.

'Look,' said Cullen, 'try not to worry about all this. I can't tell you how sorry I feel. She's a great girl . . .'

'Thanks, Tony.'

'I'll keep in touch, Alistair.'

He had given her two sleeping pills. They lay in bed in the semi-darkness. Outside the trees were moving, throwing faint, mobile shadows on the bedroom ceiling. They breathed in unison.

'What will they do?' she asked.

'Who?'

'If it's bone cancer.'

'Well . . . it depends on the type of cancer. They might have to amputate your leg.'

She lay against his chest. After a long time she said, 'And that would be it?'

'Yes, that would be it.'

He didn't tell her that even after the amputation of her leg her chances of surviving five years were less than one in four.

'How d'you fancy a one-legged wife?'

He said nothing, trying madly to conjure a flippant reply. Instead he kissed her. She laughed. 'It would make yoga easier. I can only ever get one leg crossed. I wouldn't be able to dance.'

'That makes two of us.'

She pressed closer and closed her eyes. After a while her breathing became slow and regular.

Kingsley lay on his back and watched the shadows. His unspoken doubts about Dhangi now surged forwards to haunt him. The healing touch? List the evidence: there was Henley's 'fingerprints'; there was the sensation of warmth which had once flowed from his own fingers; there were documented cures which had convinced a professor of pathology. The phenomena had ended when Dhangi had left. Proof of his complicity?

Nonsense. Kingsley managed to reach back into his former view of the world. He had observed in many of his patients how the threat of death could fertilize the most ludicrous myths and notions. His speculations were laughable.

Or had he, until now, been ignoring hard facts?

Sheila moved quietly by his side. If Cullen's diagnosis was accurate she would die before she was forty. Amputation would only delay the pain.

Maybe she didn't have cancer. Maybe the biopsy would prove otherwise. But Cullen would never have raised the subject unless he was convinced.

Dhangi, however insubstantial, was the only hope.

Kingsley did not sleep. He got up to go to the bathroom three times during the night. The rest of the time he lay on his back with his hands folded behind his head and a great vacuum in his chest. The thoughts repeated themselves, shifting this way and that, like the shadows on the bedroom ceiling.

11

Within twenty-four hours of Sheila being seen in the Infirmary, the story of her presumptive diagnosis had already reached the Douglas Calder. It accounted for the porter's solemn nod as Kingsley entered that morning, for the nurse's apologetic haste as he started his own clinic. During the coffee break he stayed in his consulting room. The domestic seemed to understand as well, as she brought him the coffee and retired backwards. Kingsley sat alone with a notepad. He looked at it for a while, then drew it towards himself and started to write: evidence for and against. He had jotted down half a dozen items when the domestic knocked on his door.

'Ready for the next patient, Mr Kingsley?'

She took his coffee. It was untouched. Kingsley crumpled the sheet of paper as she bent over his desk. Then he threw it in the bin.

He tried to persuade Sheila to take some time off school but she insisted on carrying on. She found something infinitely consoling in the history of the tea trade, long division, and that state of mind where all the tragedy of the human condition can be wrung from a grazed knee.

Two days later she went in for a bone scan. Tony Cullen showed her the result – a glossy photo of her entire skeleton. Over her right femur there was a small, bright area, apparently over exposed. Here the radioactive tracer they had injected into her blood stream was concentrated – a hot spot, probably cancer. Significantly it was the only hot spot on her skeleton. The isotope had not been concentrated elsewhere. The cancer seemed localized to one bone. There was a chance that it had not yet spread. Tony Cullen immediately booked her a bed on the ward for bone biopsy.

They gave her a private room. Kingsley came with a bunch of roses to find her already surrounded by flowers.

'Where did all these come from?'

'My school kids – they've been trooping in with vegetable produce all day. I feel like a harvest festival. How did you get these past sister?'

'What?'

'These flowers.'

'Does she object?'

'She says I can't have any more. They're supposed to reduce the oxygen in my little room.'

Kingsley forced himself to laugh. McReady shared that tenet.

'Seriously – she's going to take them all out at night and put them in the bathroom.'

'Where will you pee?'

'God knows. It's going to be pretty crowded in there.'

They continued to skirt the real issue. Kingsley picked up a label. 'Brian Oliver,' he read; 'that's not one of your kids?'

'You've not met him. He teaches English in the senior school. He said it was difficult for him to mourn for me. He said the dramatist becomes accustomed to counterfeiting all the great emotions – misery and anxiety and all that. When something really affected him he couldn't get emotional without feeling fraudulent. For people like you it's exactly the opposite. You get used to dealing objectively with tragedy. When one comes along that affects you personally, it takes you completely off guard.'

'That pompous balloon doesn't have the first idea how I . . .'

She took his hand.

'You look tired,' she said.

'Working hard.'

'No, I mean tired as if you've not slept these last couple of nights. You're not worrying are you?'

'Of course I'm worrying.'

'Don't.'

Time passed. Below their small white capsule the taxis and ambulances ferried to and from the accident centre and figures flitted between the university and the hospital. Pedestrians were straggling up the tree-lined avenue that separated the two buildings. When Kingsley stood up some students were disappearing into an archway, shouting and laughing. Their happiness seemed fantastically callous.

Kingsley drove home. Empty all day the house was perceptibly colder. He fried himself some mince, ate half of it and fell asleep in an armchair.

Sheila Kingsley was still sleepy from the premedication when they came to take her for theatre. They woke her up and she gathered after a while that she was supposed to roll onto the trolley by her bed. She did so. As she moved across, the rather inadequate theatre gown rode up over her bottom. She pulled it down again. Even after twenty-four hours in hospital she had still not got used to discarding her modesty.

They seemed to rush down the corridor. Maybe the drugs gave her a distorted impression of speed. On the ceiling, high above, the neon strip-lights raced past.

There was a clanking noise she recognized from somewhere – a lift. The spotty, disembodied face of a theatre porter loomed over her.

'You all right?'

Her mouth was dry and tacky. She found it impossible to speak. A lot of bumping, then they were off again. More people in the corridor – she was vaguely aware of their distorted shapes falling away to either side. Her trolley turned a corner and through a set of swing doors. She screwed up her eyes against the glare. When she opened them there was another face above her. She recognized that moustache. 'Richard.'

'The very same.'

'What are you doing here?'

'Well, they do let me out of the Douglas Calder now and again, strictly on parole. I thought if you had to have an anaesthetic, it might as well be the home team. Alistair came to see you this morning but apparently you were asleep. He'll be late this afternoon. There's a meeting of the management committee. How do you feel?'

'Pretty good, I've got a dry mouth. You look all blurred.'

'All right, don't get personal. I'm just going to give you a little prick, as we doctors say.'

She smiled. Behind her head Richard Short was already rummaging in the shelves for a butterfly needle. He drew up a syringe of thiopentone. The needle slipped into a vein on the back of her hand.

'This'll knock you out. Tell me if you feel anything.'

'Just a singing stench . . . a sing . . . a singing . . .' she said.

The stinging sensation crept up her arm. She forgot why she was trying to describe it. Her eyes closed.

'Nitrous on,' said Short.

He gave her a few lungfuls of nitrous from the mask, then uncoupled her from the anaesthetic machine. They wheeled her into theatre. Two porters lifted her onto the operating couch. Her leg was painted and draped. Anthony Cullen cut down to the bone. Then he started the drill.

Kingsley sat in the hospital boardroom. It had been built in an age when administration was still regarded as the occupation of the higher echelons, and even the modern light fittings could not undermine its heavy opulence. A portrait of Douglas Calder stared down from the panelled wall opposite Kingsley. It had been executed as late signs of syphilis began to distort his noble features, corrugating his brow and lending his stare a grim, accusing overtone. Kingsley chose not to look at it. He gazed through the chandelier, observing instead the continuing struggle between his intellect and his conscience.

Funding for Mukesh's research had temporarily scotched plans to close the hospital. The committee had now plunged into the trivia of hospital running with renewed enthusiasm. Kingsley, as chairman, was dimly aware of the issues: modernization of the staff cloakroom, reopening Bowman ward . . . he looked at his watch.

At four o'clock he was called to the phone.

There was a chamber between the great hall and the boardroom occupied by three red plush chairs and a telephone. Kingsley picked up the receiver and stood looking out over the cobbled road between the wrestling hall and the betting shop. A small troupe of ragged-haired kids were tossing fireworks into the water.

'Alistair?'

'Yes, hello Tony.'

Cullen cleared his throat, then plunged on. 'We did Sheila's biopsy this morning. They examined it straight away. I'm afraid it's bone cancer all right – quite a nasty one, a chondrosarcoma.'

'Yes,' said Kingsley.

'I don't know how you feel about it but I think we should go ahead with the amputation pretty soon.'

From behind the closed door, Kingsley could just hear the muffled voices of the management committee discussing canteen prices and nurses' uniforms.

Cullen said, 'The treatment of choice would be to disarticulate her hip. That minimizes the risk of recurrence from tumour which has already spread within the bone.'

'Disarticulation.'

'That's right. The artificial limb would strap around her waist; you'll have seen that kind of thing.'

'Yes.' Kingsley had seen that kind of thing. 'What about chemotherapy?'

'Only as an adjunct. The only hope of cure is amputation.'

Kingsley looked out onto the street. Seagulls bundled and fussed over the harbour water. He saw now that the children were throwing them firecrackers wrapped in bread. The gulls waited until the booby traps had exploded then swooped down for the pickings.

'We'd like to operate in, say, three or four days; might as well keep her in hospital.'

'Sure, sure,' said Kingsley. 'Thanks. I'll talk to you.'

'. . . I'm sorry it's turned out like this.'

'That's OK Tony, goodbye.'

He replaced the receiver carefully. Behind the oak doors of the committee room the conversation continued. He could recognize the voices: Frazer's Ayrshire semi-tones, McReady's Highland skirl.

He forced himself to confront his own immediate dilemma. The hours of sleeplessness had clarified nothing. The crazy Indian he had once met in the Carriage Bar now, in fact, seemed less substantial than ever. Kingsley retained little more than sketchy memories of their conversation. Dhangi was, however, responsible for the tiny seed of mystical belief that had implanted itself so perniciously in his mind. In the end, he rationalized, it was only by confronting Dhangi in the flesh that he could ever be completely free of him. With these thoughts in mind he dialled his own extension.

'Hello, Rhona. Can you do me a favour, get hold of Personnel and ask them if they have a record of a chap called Dhangi.'

'In what context?'

'He may have applied for a job here. If they don't have any record of him, then phone round the district hospitals. You know, the Western, the Eastern, the City, Bangour, Fife — maybe he's applied there. I just want his address.'

'Have you tried the medical register?'

'He's not in it. I'm not even sure he's qualified.'

'When did he apply?'

'About a month ago.'

'Are you going to offer him a job?'

'I . . . well . . . I don't know right now, I just wanted to contact him, so if you'd just do that little thing for me . . .'

'You sound worried. Is it terribly important?'

'Yes, crucial.'

'Why don't you get the police to trace him?'

Kingsley was silent. 'It's not a police case,' he said at length, embarrassed by his own deviousness. He was looking out of the window, watching Cranley limp across the street. He could envy Cranley. There was a man who could never be entangled in abstract dilemmas, whose sense of reality was as unshakeable as his daily routine. That thin black gaberdine, straight and inflexible as the spine of a Bible, seemed to represent all the rectitude and conviction which Kingsley had somehow misplaced.

Sheila was sleeping when he entered her hospital room. Kingsley sat beside her bed and stroked her forehead. The eyes opened slowly, then her head turned and she focused on his face. Her lips moved, she swallowed some bitter mucus and grimaced. Kingsley stretched out and angled the bedside light away from her face. 'How do you feel?'

'I've slept most of the time,' she said.

'Leg sore?'

'Not much – they give me injections.'

'You know what they found . . .?' he asked.

'Yes.'

'I . . .'

She reached out and touched him. 'It's all right, really it's all right. It's what I expected.'

The street droned in the distance.

'They'll amputate next week,' she said. 'Tony said three days.'

'I know. Kingsley stroked her earlobe with the back of one finger. 'But I don't want them to.'

'I know you don't, but don't be sad. I'll get over it.'

'No, I mean I'm not going to let them operate on you.'

A frown crossed her brow. 'But Tony said . . .'

'I want you to come out of the hospital tomorrow. Come home.'

She grimaced, shifting position. 'You can't be serious, darling. I've got cancer. You know about cancer. The longer you have it the worse it gets. They'll operate in a couple of days. Tony's got it all planned.'

'I'll talk to him.'

She recognized his tone and changed the subject.

'You managing at home?'

'Yes.'

'Eating all right?'

'Yes.'

'Remember to put the clocks back.'

'I'll try to.'

The problem of tracing Dhangi had continued to ferment in the back of his mind. Now, walking back through the echoing black-and-white tiled corridors, an idea bubbled to the surface. The Health Service had its own facilities for tracing people confidentially. Kingsley turned on his heel and walked back through the length of the hospital. The Department of Venereology occupied a high, turreted block at its west end. At the deserted reception desk Kingsley scribbled a quick note, sealed it, and left it for the attention of Dr Elspeth Stevenson.

When he came the next day Sheila looked better, sitting up in bed surrounded by new foliage. The 'Get Well' cards were now falling off the edges of her bedside closet; Kingsley could see the children's messages, hand-crayoned in round, telescoping letters. The pain-killers still slurred her speech.

As he left, the sister cornered him.

'Can you pop into the office a minute, Mr Kingsley? Mr Cullen wants to have a word with you before you go.'

'Hello Tony.'

Cullen returned a rather anaemic smile and closed the door. They were alone now.

'I think we should talk this over, Alistair . . . I think you're making a mistake.'

Kingsley leant back against the desk. 'You don't want me to take her home yet?'

'I want to amputate.'

Kingsley studied the parquet flooring. Tony Cullen's hands were in the pockets of his capacious grey suit. A solid shelf abdomen hung over the waistband. He jingled some change in his pockets. His voice softened. 'Consider if she was any other patient . . .'

'She's not any other patient.'

'I just can't see what you're looking to gain by delaying. The diagnosis is indisputable. She knows that leg's got to come off. If you take her home she's just going to brood about it. Psychologically it's easiest for her if we bash on. She'll adjust to it after the operation – they do.'

'I don't care about what *they* do, Tony, we're talking about my wife.'

Cullen remained impassive.

'I'm sorry,' said Kingsley.

'That's OK. I can imagine what you're going through – I think I can. If Carole got something like this I'd be up the wall. But you've got to face it, man. There's no sense in delaying the inevitable.'

He studied Kingsley's face. 'The inevitable, Alistair. I hope you're not banking on anything coming from that research down your way. If there's anything in that it's going to take months to come to the surface. You know that.'

'Of course I know that. I just want time to think a few things over. Anyway, my research worker Dr Mukesh is on study leave – we won't be pushing back the frontiers of science again until mid-November.'

Cullen smiled at the joke. His face flattened again. 'I'll tell you what I'm afraid of. The drugs we can give her for this are pretty primitive. They'll knock her for six and they're no guarantee against further invasion. If we allow that tumour to spread into the head we'll need to take half her pelvis away. You've seen results of that.'

'Yes, I've seen that.'

'It's not a pleasant operation.'

'Give me four weeks.'

'That's maximum,' said Cullen.

12

Kingsley had always thought it rather appropriate that the Chambers Street staff-club should be situated adjacent to both the Students' Union and the Museum. In atmosphere it fitted rather neatly between the libertine chaos of the one and the reverent silence of the other. It had been recarpeted since his last visit and the modern art on the walls had been replaced with new, but equally anonymous paintings. Above the rubber plants and groups of armchairs there hung the buzz of earnest conversation, punctuated by the forcibly suppressed cries of other people's children.

Elspeth Stevenson had arrived before him. She had entrenched herself in a corner behind a copy of *The Times* from where she was sending up smoke signals.

Kingsley tipped the newspaper gently and she looked up. 'Alistair!' she exclaimed, extinguishing the cigarette butt. 'So nice to get your note. Nobody takes me out to lunch any more. Do you want to get yourself a drink?'

'I won't bother.'

'Of course,' she said, 'I don't suppose you can do your job after a couple of these.' She took a liberal swig from her own glass of gin. 'Personally, I can't do mine without them.'

Kingsley smiled. 'You're an evil lady.'

'I'd like to create that impression.' Elspeth Stevenson ran a hand through her hair – silver-grey but for a strand in the front stained yellow by nicotine. 'Unfortunately I no longer have the equipment.' She nodded to a passing colleague then fell serious. 'Bloody bad news about Sheila,' she said, 'bloody bad. I rang up that butcher Cullen and told him to put away his hacksaw till he'd had a second opinion. You poor thing, Alistair. You must be shattered. Hell, if I had legs like Sheila's I'd be shattered.' She lifted up the hem of her tweed suit. 'If Tony Cullen wants a leg he can have this one. Christ knows nobody else wants it.'

'Thanks for the offer, Elspeth.'

'It's the least I can do.' She scrutinized him closely. 'You look bloody tired, Alistair, you poor soul. You must be worried sick. It's the pits isn't it. Headmistress of mine used to say, just before she beat the living daylights out of us – the old pervert – she used to say "Stevenson – only the good die young". She was right, too. I've got a long life ahead of me. I'm sorry, I talk too much. Here, have a cigarette.'

'No thanks.'

'I forgot, you smoke a pipe don't you.' Dr Stevenson lit another cigarette with a slim gold lighter and inhaled furiously. 'I only smoke these things to make my patients feel at ease. Half of them are so crippled by guilt by the time they get to the department. It must be a great relief to find a degenerate old bag like me at the helm instead of a real doctor. You still golfing?'

'I've not played for a few weeks.'

'I have. That bugger Richard Short gave me a round the other day. His game has gone to pieces. He insisted on bringing his new woman along. I took four holes off him. He couldn't keep his eyes off her tits. Nice enough girl though. Have you met her?'

'She's my secretary.'

'Is she? No wonder you look so tired.' Stevenson paused, looking for a response. 'Cheer up, Alistair. When I was a girl it was considered bloody rude not to laugh at other people's jokes.' Kingsley smiled.

'Mind you,' said Elspeth Stevenson, 'at that time it wasn't considered very ladylike to want to be a doctor, nor to smoke these things.' She regarded the cigarette soberly. 'I've spent my life struggling against convention. Now, when I should be cashing in on it, I find that everyone else is behaving the same way.

There you go. I'm not even very amusing any more. And I talk about myself too much.'

Kingsley patted her knee. 'Do you want to eat?'

'Certainly,' she said, 'but not in that upstairs place. It's full of sweaty squash players and infants falling on their arses.'

'Fine,' said Kingsley. 'We'll eat downstairs.' He helped her to her feet. The downstairs restaurant was twice as expensive as the canteen, but in compensation it was half as crowded and a good deal less noisy.

As they started on the second course, Kingsley steered Elspeth Stevenson around to the subject of her work.

'Young people never fail to impress me,' she confessed. 'I had a Swiss girl in yesterday who'd been in the country for two weeks and claimed to have fifteen contacts.'

'That's what I wanted to talk to you about.'

'You were one of them?'

'No. Contacts. I need to trace a chap. I wondered how to go about it.'

Stevenson loaded her steak with mustard, then popped it in her mouth.

'Who is he sleeping with?'

'No one,' said Kingsley.

'Come on,' Stevenson swallowed and sipped at her wine. 'Everyone's sleeping with someone . . . Except me,' she added on reflection.

'Just consider he's not sleeping with anyone.'

'Well he wouldn't be a patient of mine, Alistair. All our work is done on a postal basis. We ask about contacts then send them all a letter. It's a bit like the chain letters kids used to send to each other. You know, write to the six named on this postcard or all sorts of horrible things might happen to you.' She paused. 'With VD they sometimes do.'

Kingsley refilled her wine glass. 'That's a dead loss then,' he said. 'How else can I find the bloke?'

'What do you want to find him for?'

'I'd rather not tell you.'

Dr Stevenson looked at him over the top of her spectacles. 'I must say, Alistair, this is all very untypical. I always regarded you as a champion of honesty and open dealing. You're not contemplating a crime of passion.'

Kingsley laughed at the idea.

'I'm sorry to disappoint you, Elspeth. It's actually quite mundane. I just want to find a chap who I've only met once and I don't know how to go about it.'

'Well, you should get the police to help you. They're good at that kind of thing.'

Kingsley chewed ruminatively. 'The problem is,' he said eventually, 'I don't have any good reason for putting them to the trouble.'

'So lie to them,' said Stevenson happily. 'There's all sorts of medical reasons for wanting to find a chap. Tell them he's a typhoid carrier.'

'Now the one thing I don't want to start,' Kingsley told her, 'is a national crisis.'

Dr Stevenson agreed that the idea had its drawbacks and they dropped the subject. Over dessert he allowed her to reminisce about her continental relatives and their ill-fated attempts to sabotage her first marriage. But Kingsley found his mind flitting backwards at intervals to her suggestion for tracing Dhangi. The principle was basically sound. After they parted, he phoned to ask Jennings to start the list alone, and drove back via the central police station, an unimposing white office block on the edge of Inverleith park. The duty sergeant ushered him into a small, bare room with a window occupying one wall. Beyond the playing fields the delicate Gothic spires of his old school rose above the trees. Kingsley had no particularly fond memories of the place, but recently, driving past, he had felt more sentimental about it than he could ever previously recall. In comparison with his present situation, even recent events had taken on a halcyon, almost mythical quality – golf with Richard Short, that night on the hospital roof. Six weeks ago. It already seemed much more distant.

Inspector Cairney came in wearing a sheepskin jacket. He was a brisk, serious man with ruddy cheeks and a quiff of black hair across his forehead.

'Take a seat, Mr Kingsley.'

Kingsley moved away from the window and sat at the table. The inspector sat down opposite him. 'Now,' he said, 'I believe you're looking for this fellow who might have contracted . . .' – here he looked at the notepad in his hand – 'Hepatitis B.'

'That's right,' Kingsley told him.

'What is it?' said Cairney. 'Anything serious?'

'It can be.' Having embarked on the lie, Kingsley found that the specialist information at his disposal lent it a disconcerting ring of truth. 'It's an occupational hazard in the profession. It might be transmitted by the careless handling of blood samples. We've just learnt that a patient recently under investigation was a carrier of the disease. Dr Dhangi only visited our hospital briefly, but you can't be too careful.'

'No,' said Cairney. 'I dare say you can't.' He tipped back in his seat, leaning precariously against the plate glass of the window. 'My problem is this,' he said at length. 'I appreciate your concern over Dr Dhangi and obviously you need to get hold of him somehow, but contrary to popular belief it's very difficult to put your finger on someone who doesn't have a criminal record. We don't have a hell of a lot to go on.' Cairney itemized the points on his short fingers. 'You say he probably doesn't have a car, so Swansea won't be able to help us. He doesn't live locally, or have a fixed abode that you know of. He's foreign but, again, immigration don't really keep very close tabs on people. And you say your secretary's drawn a blank with both the British Medical Association and the local hospitals.' Cairney blew out his cheeks and showed Kingsley his square palms.

'Fair enough.' Kingsley's disappointment was tempered by relief. He had no talent for deception and was not enjoying it.

'Here's what I'll do,' said Cairney. 'I'll get one of our chaps to spend all day on the phone tomorrow ringing round the health services. It's possible your doctor left a forwarding address with someone else before he arrived here. There's one other possibility. If you come up with a description we'll mail it to places he might visit in Edinburgh, Indian restaurants and so on. I'm afraid that's the best I can do.'

'I appreciate it,' Kingsley said. 'Who do I give the description to?'

'We'll give you an identikit – see what you can do with that.'

'Thank you.'

Cairney left and returned shortly afterwards with a black box. Kingsley set to work with the strips of card but already his memory of Dhangi's features was clouded and obscure. He found a pair of hollowed cheeks which corresponded with his memory. He found a hooked nose and a pair of full lips. However, the final effect looked no more like Dhangi than any other face. Out of interest he attempted to construct a replica of Richard Short. At that point Cairney returned.

Cairney looked down at the table. 'Is that him?'

'No. I was just experimenting. It's an anaesthetist friend of mine.'

'Looks like a bloody psychopath.'

'He is.'

Kingsley made up for his lost time by working late at the hospital. He drove home that evening through the centre of town, over Hanover Street, then down past the floodlit art gallery, climbing again in the short, sweeping rise to the city's oldest quarter, a random conglomerate of bridges, cobbled lanes and endless black steps crammed into the Gothic contours of Castle Hill. He considered that in going to the police he could well have driven Dhangi further underground. In a city such as this a man could hide forever.

13

Four days later Inspector Cairney called in at the hospital. Rhona showed him through to Kingsley's office, still wearing the sheepskin coat. It was cold outside and the filamentous blood vessels which traversed the inspector's cheeks were picked out in sharp relief. His eyes wandered round the office as he shook hands with Kingsley.

'I won't trouble you for long,' he said. 'Not much to report, but I've got some stuff here which might help.' Cairney picked up the Iona marble paperweight and examined it as he talked. 'I got in touch with immigration. They had a record of a Dr Acharya Dhangi who arrived here in April. Qualified pathologist. Working visit. Temporary resident's visa renewed once.' He looked up. 'Unfortunately there was no forwarding address.'

From outside there came a loud explosion, followed by a burst of hysterical children's laughter. Cairney walked to the window.

'It's good of you to make the effort,' said Kingsley.

'All part of the job,' said Cairney. 'Keeps me off the street. Liable to get blown up this time of year. Anyway,' he said, returning the stone to the edge of Kingsley's desk, 'the hospital phone calls were quite productive. He gets about, your Dr Dhangi. Since he arrived here he's been doing locum work all over the place.' Cairney returned to his notepad. 'Listen to this. He's worked in Brighton General Hospital for three weeks, Royal Southants for two . . . couple of weeks at Torbay Hospital in Devon, then on to Southmead Hospital in Bristol.' Cairney scanned down the list. 'Liverpool . . . Kingston General Hospital in Hull . . . Collingwood Clinic in Newcastle . . . ended up just recently at the Gartnavel General Hospital in Glasgow. That's just from tracing the references he gave. Never left a forwarding address, just headed off and popped up somewhere else a week later. Looks as though he was doing a tour of coastal Britain.' Cairney pocketed the notebook. 'So there you are. If you're really worried about him I'd just get your administration to put a circular round the hospital service. He'll probably turn up somewhere new in the next couple of weeks.'

Kingsley forced a look of optimism. 'Thank you,' he said, 'that's very helpful.'

'Well,' said Cairney, 'it's not a lot, but there's a good chance you'll find him.'

Rhona showed the detective out and Kingsley was left to gaze out of the window. He had no delusions that Dhangi would be moving on. The itinerant pattern validated the Indian's original story. And he claimed to have found what he was looking for in Leith. Also, on a much less rational level, there remained the feeling that Dhangi was nearby, deliberately out of reach. It was nothing more than an instinct, a premonition.

Since when had he believed in premonitions?

Chandra Mukesh was similarly unwilling to rely on his instincts and could think of several rational explanations for the vague paranoia which had beset him since the beginning of his study leave. A primary consideration was the fact that he had been obliged to spend the last three evenings in the airless library of the Douglas Calder poring over journals on immunology. Now, as he pulled the door closed and clattered down the fire-escape, the sense of impending disaster returned to plague him. He gripped the handle of his briefcase and focused his mind on the prospect of his research project. He still had no friends to speak of in Edinburgh, but his old colleagues in Manchester would be mightily impressed.

He was coming to the bottom of the steps. He still had to negotiate the narrow alley to Causeway Lane. He resolved that he would not have to run along it tonight. He slowed consciously and kept his eyes straight ahead, not noticing the gob of betel-stained saliva on the bottom step. He thought of his parents. He thought of Calcutta. He thought of winter in Kashmir. He thought of his sister in Bombay. Of her husband. Of summer on Juhu beach. Of his sister's children. He heard a sound and whirled around too late. Something exploded inside his skull and he crumpled to the ground.

That evening the Kingsleys had been invited out for cocktails in the New Town. Richard Short was there with Rhona, consorting quite openly now, but Short's displays of affection had a manic quality which suggested she had still not agreed to sleep with him. Kingsley managed to joke and banter with him. Everyone knew about Sheila's illness now and he realized they were making allowances for his ill-concealed neurosis. Sheila seemed to be coping well but when they were separated he noticed her public postures for the first time. She tended to keep the right leg crossed behind her left, or angled slightly to the side, or folded beneath her when she sat, as if she was now denying its presence.

They left early. The first round of anti-cancer injections had sapped Sheila's energy and now caused her increasingly frequent bouts of nausea. Driving home he looked across to her. Her face was contorted with pain. She noticed him looking at her and forced a smile.

When they got home she took two sleeping tablets and went to bed. Kingsley sat downstairs with the lights out, gazing out of the front window and listening to the trees. Dhangi was beginning to obsess him. He had now admitted to himself that Dhangi's outlandish claims may conceivably be valid, that he could convey, indeed had conveyed, the healing touch. In previously dismissing Dhangi, he had ignored, by his own mental inflexibility, a medical advance of astounding proportions. He had to find Dhangi not only for Sheila's sake but also to allay this growing sense of guilt.

He knew two things about Dhangi as a social animal: that he drank and that something attracted him to the dockland. He would begin his search with the Carriage Bar.

He left early the following evening, leaving Jennings to finish the operating list. As he passed the children's ward a nurse was putting paper Hallowe'en decorations on the windows. Outside, Harbour Lane smelt of cordite.

At five minutes past opening time the regulars had already colonized the Carriage Bar – strung out along the dark counter in a thin, disconsolate line.

At length he caught the woman's attention.

'What will it be then?'

'I'm looking for an Indian chap called Dhangi.'

'Have you looked around?'

'I don't see him just now.'

'Well, he's not here then.'

She was called away to pull another couple of pints. Kingsley eventually retrieved her. 'I wondered if you knew the name.'

'What name?'

'Dhangi.'

'No, I don't know anyone called that.'

Someone put ten pence in the jukebox. Kingsley shouted above the noise. 'Maybe your husband knows him?'

The woman set her mouth in exasperation and called, 'Ronald, d'you know a customer called Dhangi?'

'Dhangi who?'

'That's his surname.'

'Never heard of him,' said the husband, without looking up. She made as if to leave. Kingsley reached across and grabbed her arm.

'Listen,' he said, 'I met him in here a while back. He usually wears a dark suit. His name's Achara ... something like that ... Dhangi. If you get him in here, can you give him this.'

Kingsley handed her his card; she looked at it, then back at Kingsley.

'You a surgeon?'

'Yes.'

She looked across to her husband. 'Hey, Ronald, this one's a surgeon from the hospital.'

Ronald laughed, revealing his stained teeth. 'Carriage Bar's going up in the world.'

Kingsley left. Out on the street again the cold air pinched through his suit. He would return later and the next evening if necessary. Meanwhile there was the Anchor, the Sutton and the Duke.

For the next few days there was an effigy outside the hospital railings – an old jersey stuffed with newspaper. The head was a deflated leather football crowned with seaweed, the legs a limp pair of flannel trousers. The children who had made it would install themselves at three o'clock and start hustling the bus queue for pennies for the Guy. To Kingsley the leather face was a hideous parody of Dhangi's. He often saw Dhangi now. He saw Dhangi as a castaway sees mirages of land. Dhangi's face hung above him each morning as he lay on his back with Sheila moving restlessly beside him. Dhangi occupied the silence in his car on the way to work, and the dishevelled pathologist seemed to adopt the form of countless strangers, glimpsed in the bus queue, followed down the lane by the wrestling hall, tapped on the shoulder outside the Co-op. It was never Dhangi – just another vision to torment him.

At the Douglas Calder his waiting list began to lengthen. He left work at five-thirty each evening and returned home four hours later smelling of beer and cigarette smoke.

He was not aware of 5 November. His calendar was now

drastically simplified to a record of the days available before Cullen's deadline. Richard Short, on the other hand, took advantage of the date to hold an impromptu barbecue in the gardens outside his flat. The high Georgian terraces stood back in silent disapproval as Short nipped backwards and forwards with a fish slice, turning the steaks and orchestrating the firework display. He had strung light bulbs round the trees. Above them the sky over the New Town was ripped with rushing, blossoming fire. Elspeth Stevenson helped herself to the punch. 'Did you invite Alistair Kingsley?'

'He said he wasn't free.' Short nibbled at the hot corner of a piece of steak. 'He's been a bit off recently.'

Elspeth Stevenson moved round to Short's side of the fire, shielding her eyes against the smoke. 'He's just worried about his wife.'

'No, really, he's different now.'

'He's just worried,' she told him.

At that moment Kingsley was hunched over a table in the Purple Rose tavern. He was in much the same position an hour later when he was woken by a persistently ringing bell which penetrated his confused dreams like an awl. He raised his head from his arms and looked up blearily.

'Time, please.'

'Sorry?'

'Drink up now.'

The barman was impatiently clearing glasses from the circular table where Kingsley's head had rested and hooking them over his fingers. He produced a cloth and tapped impatiently on Kingsley's arm.

'Lift.'

Kingsley lifted his arms and found there was still a glass in his right hand. It was empty.

'I'll take that.'

'Thank you,' he muttered thickly.

'Thank you and good night,' the barman replied without sympathy, moving on to clear the next table.

The bell continued to ring. Kingsley belched. His own breath smelt of acetone and there was an unpleasant sweet taste in his mouth. He shuffled along the plastic bench until a space presented itself, then hoisted himself uncertainly to his feet. An area of stained glass resolved itself into the pub's door and Kingsley projected himself towards it, leaning on people and chair backs where they came within range. The door swung open and he stumbled out. Even after it had closed behind him the bell continued to echo in his ears. He staggered against some railings and fumbled to relieve himself, meanwhile taking great lungfuls of cold air. He remembered to feel for his wallet. It was still there. Bending forwards again to button his fly he encountered a searing pain in the middle of his forehead. When he straightened it subsided. The car keys were still in his pocket but he had no recollection of where he had left the car.

Supporting himself on the railings, he squinted at the black tenements which rose on either side but recognized no landmark. The slums extended outwards in every direction, a dark web of streets and side streets bearing little relation to any conceivable street plan. Kingsley chose a direction at random and set off down it, making a conscious effort to avoid colliding with the wall on his left. The next intersection he reached was no more recognizable than the first. Kingsley chose another street and bowled down it, zigzagging between the irregularly spaced pools of lamplight. He arrived at a crippled phone box and leant against it to regain his breath. The endless ramifications of the black maze seemed to multiply on every side.

'Dhangi,' he muttered as he set off again.

A car appeared out of nowhere in a blast of light and deafening noise. He felt his way around the front of the bonnet. A door opened and someone shouted an obscenity at him, then it was gone and Kingsley was running, stumbling down a narrow black alley, his eyes fixed on the concentric haloes of a distant light. The caustic air seemed to condense at the back of his throat and drip into his chest. He kept his weight forwards and his feet moved automatically beneath him. 'Dhangi, Dhangi,' they repeated on the cobbles.

He emerged into an octagonal courtyard. The single white street lamp at its centre was surrounded by a few vandalized saplings. Kingsley stumbled across and hung exhausted against it. 'Dhangi,' he mumbled, then, raising his head, 'Dhangi!' he shouted at the vacant sky. His words rebounded from the blinded buildings on every side. The lamp-post seemed to sway and topple like the mast of a sinking ship. 'Dhangi!' he called again, clinging to it grimly. 'Can you hear me? . . . You win! . . . OK? . . . I need you . . . I believe you!'

He listened for a reply but heard only echoes of his own voice. Gradually the lamp-post righted itself, the alcohol momentarily deserted him and he cradled his fuddled, aching head in his hands.

When, in the small grey hours, he finally found his car, there was an ugly orange scratch running down one side and the wing mirror had been bent sideways. Kingsley climbed in painfully and drove home in a dream. He still had thirteen days.

At the hospital he recognized that attitudes towards him were changing. William, the porter, would give him a solemn nod as he entered and left. Jennings seemed keen to take over more and more of the operating responsibility. McReady seldom joked with him and patients who once knew him well now regarded him with uncertain deference.

November gathered momentum.

Now they rarely talked over breakfast. Outside, the front garden was almost naked; just a few limp leaves remained on the chestnut tree, like the flags of a defeated army. Sheila picked at a bowl of cornflakes. Her face was thinner. She looked up and met her husband's eyes, pulled the dressing-gown tighter and leant forwards. Her eyes were still puffy from sleep and her hair fell over her forehead. She pushed it back with one hand.

'I got my appointment yesterday. Five days.'

'That's good.' His words had the shallow, evasive joviality of an outgoing politician. She noticed how, over the past week, the area around his eyes had become blotched and lined.

'You've got a mark on your collar.'

Kingsley fingered it idly. He left for work without changing it.

That afternoon there was a note from Rhona on his desk:

'MR CRANLEY CALLED. DR MUKESH'S LOCUM LEFT YESTER-DAY. MUKESH NOT BACK FROM STUDY LEAVE. CAN'T CONTACT HIM AT HOME. HAVE RUNG PERSONNEL.'

The ultimate irony. Mukesh late back from leave, depriving them of a pathologist in the immediate future. He crumpled the note and returned to the more pressing issue. Five days. He rang up the Infirmary and caught Tony Cullen between operations. Cullen had been trying to contact him.

'Bit of bad news, Alistair. The review X-ray shows a percep-tible increase in the size of Sheila's tumour. It's growing faster than I anticipated. Not to worry though. She's on the list for Tuesday.'

'I'm sorry, Tony, it's not going to be long enough.'

There was a stupefied silence, then – 'What do you mean, not long enough?'

'I want you to postpone the operation again.'

'For Jesus' sake Alistair, you can't be serious. The woman's in increasing pain. She's already drugged to the eyelids to no effect. You're asking me to sit back and wait for that tumour to kill her.'

'Just put it off, Tony.'

'Give me one good reason.'

'Because I ask you.'

'You've got to be mad. Have you asked Sheila what she wants?'

'She'll go along with me.'

120

'Just wait . . . just wait a minute. I don't know if you understand the situation. This is a highly malignant tumour. I'm losing time every day.'

'My time,' said Kingsley.

'It's not your bloody time. The woman's putting up with the pain just to make you feel better. To what end? Nothing. You both look like ghosts. Sheila being poisoned and you happily banging nails into her coffin . . . Alistair, are you still there?'

'Yes, I'm still here.'

'The longer you wait the less chance she has of living. That's hard fact.'

Kingsley considered that. Another hard fact presented itself: not having found Dhangi to date he was unlikely to come across him in the next few weeks.

Cullen interrupted the silence.

'She'll come in Monday for a pre-op workup – I'll operate Wednesday. OK?'

'OK,' he said.

In front of the social security the road widened into a triangle of cobblestones, bounded on one side by the wrestling hall and on another by the street-level harbour water. There was a long wooden bench where the alcoholics sat, their backs to the harbour. It was a cold day but they were still there, an ill-fitting collection of coats and half mitts. They swigged from a collection of bottles, largely meths in milk. Between drinks they would talk in short, ponderous exchanges, cough, and watch the social security. Occasionally one would toss a bottle over his head, now arcing through the crystal air to fall with a muffled splash into the dead harbour waters. The ripples spread outwards, continuing, still perceptible, to the warehouse opposite. They spread over the flat black waters, and five minutes later the ripples were gone, only the half-submerged neck of one more bottle gaping from the water like a feeding bird.

Just below the bridge something disturbed the sweep of the

spreading wave – a smooth, round object about the size of a half-submerged melon. A dock worker saw it as he crossed the bridge. Something in the shape of this floater made him stop and take a second look. It was not a melon, nor even a football. Looking into the murky water he realized with a sudden horror that the tatty fronding from its upper surface might conceivably be human hair.

By lunchtime a line of pedestrians had strung out in a broken necklace along the edge of the dock. They sat on the bollards, stood champing by the railings and leaned, one foot cocked backwards, against the wall of the social security. The traffic had been diverted and the bridge was shut off by police barricades. Two police cars had arranged themselves within the enclosures. The frogmen stood around stamping their feet as the winch was set up on the balustrade, then both lowered themselves slowly into the water.

Even from a distance the object they fished out of the harbour was distinguishable as a man's corpse, or at least part of a man's corpse. The body had been somehow severed in a crude diagonal line from one armpit to the opposite groin. The frogmen had attached a rope around its middle. Now, as they raised it on the winch, the torso dipped abruptly, head down, arms extended. A ripple of disgust spread round the spectators. Water ran from the ears and the mouth and the reddened, patchy hair. When they swung it on to the bridge one of the men posted to receive it turned away; the other cupped a hand over his nose and mouth. Close to, what skin that remained was mottled purple and yellow; the clothes had largely rotted away, as had the hair and eyes. The lopsided mouth gaped open, locked solid.

The corpse was transported for forensic examination at the Infirmary. From the dental pattern they identified it conclusively as that of Chandra Mukesh.

14

There was a rolled-up newspaper protruding from the pocket of Cairney's sheepskin coat. As he sat down opposite Kingsley he took it out and put it on the desk between them. During their interview two uniformed policemen walked past his office window. The hospital was alive with blue uniforms. In the mortuary two policemen were grilling Cranley on Mukesh's movements prior to his disappearance. Cranley's sparse responses to their questions fell between the sucking and clattering of his false teeth. Cranley had seen a lot of death and mutilation, but the reports of the state of Mukesh's body had affected him. Now he didn't want to talk about it. He regarded a lot of the questioning from police and reporters alike as a desecration.

Kingsley, similarly, had little to offer. He felt embarrassed by his ignorance of Mukesh. It highlighted how, over the past few weeks, he had perhaps been neglecting his duties as chief consultant. And there was a deeper, less tangible discomfort: an immediate sense of his own guilt.

Inspector Cairney had treated the whole thing with his customary buoyancy.

'Appreciate your help, Mr Kingsley.' He slotted the black leather notebook back into his inside pocket. 'Even the little pieces count – like cuisenaire rods. Did you ever have them? No? Well, nice seeing you again.'

He made as if to go, then turned back, took the newspaper, and held up the front page.

CANCER PIONEER IN BRUTAL MURDER SCARE – *Roland Spears reports.*

'If you have to speak to Mukesh's relatives again, I'd play this kind of thing down. No real reason to suspect anything sinister. Personally, I think the fellow might just have had a few drinks, fallen in the harbour, then got caught in the mechanism of the swing bridge. It happens. We had one of those five years ago, remember?'

'Yes, I do.'

'Good. I think that should be the official line.' He turned to the door. As he reached the handle he turned back once more. 'D'you ever find that whatsisname, that other pathologist, the chap who'd been exposed to that virus?'

'No, I never did.'

Cairney turned up one corner of his mouth. 'Pity,' he remarked, 'you could probably use him now.'

Kingsley spent the weekend at home digging the garden, working around the borders, straining and wrestling with the cold, black earth. The work was therapy, mindless. The shock of Mukesh's death became absorbed into the crushed despondency with which he regarded his lost chance with Dhangi, the inevitability of Sheila's operation and the loss of the personal qualities on which his self-esteem was founded. In his pursuit of Dhangi he had burnt all the sacraments of his upbringing – personal dignity, emotional restraint and professional objectivity. Now, without Dhangi, he was a Faust who had sold his soul and been given nothing in exchange.

Tuesday morning: Sheila had been admitted the day before for a transfusion of blood and platelets. Kingsley lay in bed until six-thirty, then dressed and made himself some cornflakes and toast. The whole procedure, the placing of the cup in saucer, the assimilation of milk and coffee, and sugar, the washing of the few dishes and the sweeping of the crumbs from the table, seemed infinitely small and tedious.

He was early this morning and the roads were even quieter

than usual. He switched on the radio, to some amiable Radio Forth presenter who could drown out the outside world with his fatuous chatter. A rash of weed was breaking the surface of Blackford pond. The hill behind lay in a damp, black eiderdown of mist and foliage. He negotiated the new by-pass round the university precinct and passed the Infirmary, heavily aware of Sheila's presence there, like the house of an ex-lover. Descending to the town centre the grey roofscape stretched northwards. A series of Georgian boulevards took him to the top of the long, straight drag northwards. It narrowed as he progressed downhill towards the estuary; the fine sandstone office blocks were crowded out by cheap-fronted shops.

He had become accustomed to the tricks played on him by his sense of hope and did not allow himself to be affected by the figure loitering outside the main entrance to the Douglas Calder. The man stood quite still with his hands limp by his sides, as Dhangi had stood. In the morning twilight his features were an indistinct blur.

Kingsley parked, took his briefcase and crossed the quad-rangle. The face looked up. Kingsley drew closer. His intestines wormed into his chest.

'You have a vacancy.' Dhangi's voice was even, betraying neither surprise nor smugness. Kingsley walked forwards. The hand which he held out to shake was trembling uncon-trollably. Their palms touched. Dhangi's cold skin had the texture of candle wax. His haunted features were suddenly familiar. But when Kingsley caught sight, beyond Dhangi's shoulder, of his own reflection in the glass of the inner door, he barely recognized the drawn, pale mask which stared back at him.

15

'I'll no work with him.'

Kingsley took his hand from his forehead. 'Take a seat, Mr Cranley.' Kingsley gestured to the vacant office chair. Cranley declined. The black suit hung from his shoulders as if from a coat hanger. His clenched hands unconsciously adopted the military configuration – thumbs foremost.

'Is there some specific reason why you dislike the man?'

Cranley said nothing, only continued to stare at a point two inches above Kingsley's head. It seemed to him that Dhangi's appointment was conclusive evidence of Kingsley's moral and mental collapse. 'He's no business here.'

'Come on now, Mr Cranley. Dr Dhangi has fine credentials. He's an experienced pathologist. He's worked . . .'

'The police are after him.'

'The police have questioned him, as they've questioned all of us, in connection with Dr Mukesh's accident. Dr Dhangi himself is above suspicion. He worked closely with the police during his appointment in Leeds. He's a good man, very bright. He was among the pathologists on one of the Ripper cases down there.'

'Aye, Mukesh was ripped.'

'Look, Mr Cranley. I know you've been with the hospital for a fair time.'

'Twenty-six years,' said Cranley.

'I can understand that you feel you should have some say in what goes on in the mortuary.'

'I've never asked much, sir.'

'I know that, I know that, Mr Cranley.' Kingsley searched

the panelled walls for inspiration. The pegboard covered in printed sheets, the rota list, the year planner, the printed fire regulations.

His gaze returned to Cranley's bony fists.

'I realize,' Kingsley looked at his own fingernails, 'I realize that Dr Dhangi may appear rather . . . neurotic. His behaviour is not, perhaps, instantly endearing . . . I know that he may not be your first choice of a workmate. But he does have a lot to contribute to the hospital . . . You'll eventually get on fine together. If Dr Dhangi appears at first rather uncommunicative, he'll still appreciate your expert advice on some aspects of dissection.' Kingsley smiled. Cranley finally abandoned the pretence of respect.

'The only expert advice that bugger will get from me . . .'

Rhona knocked and entered.

'Just leave these on the table, thanks Rhona.'

She deposited the letters in front of him. Cranley turned to watch the door snib shut. 'It's either him or me, sir.'

'I'm sorry, Mr Cranley.'

'Twenty-six years,' said Cranley.

'I don't want to lose you, Mr Cranley. You're a fine assistant. We all know that. You're necessary here.'

'But not as necessary as yon Hindoo bugger – is that it, sir?'

'Listen, Mr Cranley. I don't expect you to understand my motives, but for reasons of my own I need to employ this man Dhangi, if only short term.'

'How short term?'

'I can't say that. I can only ask you to try and tolerate him for as long as necessary.'

'I won't,' said Cranley abruptly, then his natural deference to rank won over his righteous indignation. He looked down at his knuckles, and removed them from Kingsley's desk, then wiped the green leather with the tips of his fingers. 'I'll not do it, sir. I'm sorry.'

'I don't know why you're afraid of him, Mr Cranley.'

Cranley's eyes came to focus directly on Kingsley's, bright as knives.

'I'm not afraid of that man.'

'Sorry, Mr Cranley, that wasn't intended as an insult.'

'Well, I take it as one, sir.'

'I apologize, Mr Cranley.'

Cranley rubbed at his game leg. He had been called a coward once before. 'I'm not afraid of him,' he repeated.

Kingsley was aware that he was pressing on a raw wound but he was too tired for diplomacy. 'So you'll stay with us?'

The thick, brown veins stood out from Cranley's neck.

'If he gives trouble he'll be out.'

'If he gives trouble I'll hold myself personally responsible.'

Cranley looked at him directly once more. With that, Kingsley's words became a promise. Cranley turned and left.

When he had gone, Kingsley leant back in the leather upholstered chair and pressed his own temples. He was already experiencing the sensations Dhangi's first appearance within the hospital had produced – a rawness of the muscles of his arms and legs. Once these symptoms had debilitated him. Now they were not unpleasant, almost restoring. What had worked in him then was working now.

Up at the Infirmary the sister met him in the short corridor between the doors to the main ward. She was a short, tidily kept woman with the crisp, austere features of an alabaster statuette. Her uniform was spotless. 'Hello' was all she said but her tone carried more implicit disapproval than Kingsley chose to accept from her.

'I've come to see my wife,' he said curtly.

'She's in a fair bit of pain.'

'So I gather, sister.'

The door swung shut behind him. Through the glass panel he caught sight, briefly, of the sister's face – a small pointed frown, then she was gone. He looked back down at his wife.

Sheila, grimacing, hauled herself into a sitting position.

'They say you want to delay the operation again.'

'That's right.'

She said nothing for a while. He sat on the edge of her bed and took her hand. She slipped it free. 'I'm going ahead with it.'

'Sheila . . .'

'I don't want to be kept like this any longer. I'm sick all the time. My hair's falling out. The longer you delay, the more pointless it seems. I feel like a prisoner on death row.'

'Just four more days.'

Sheila pulled herself up in bed. 'For Christ's sake, Alistair!'

The sister would have heard that. Kingsley pictured her tidy smugness.

Kingsley tugged at the blankets, tucked firmly under her mattress. He created a small vent, slipped his hand between the sheets. He found her thigh, touched and she squirmed away. He followed her, gripping her leg. Yes, he could feel it just above the knee, that same warmth. He focused on that area, rubbing, kneading the muscle. Sheila had relaxed, her eyes were on his face.

'What are you doing?'

Kingsley cleared his throat. 'Supposing I told you I could cure this . . . without an amputation, I mean.'

'You can't.'

'You remember those cases down at the Douglas Calder. Sandra Spears and all that. Remember all the stuff about a cure for cancer?'

'Yes.'

'It's true. I mean it worked then.'

'What worked then?'

'My touch,' he said. He tried to sound as matter-of-fact as possible but the pronouncement assumed a hollow melodrama of its own.

'You what?'

'I can heal by touch.'

'Alistair?' Sheila's eyes widened and filled with tears.

'Look, don't say anything, don't look at me like that. I'm not mad. I am not mad. There's this man. He's called Dhangi. He's a pathologist. He came to the hospital a long while back. I told you about him. He met me in the car park outside the Douglas Calder. All he wanted was a job in the mortuary. That's when it all started, the strange pathology reports. Dhangi said they were his doing. He said he'd conveyed some kind of healing touch on me. I didn't believe him. I thought he was completely cracked. Believe me, I did. I've tried not to believe in him. But now . . . now it seems I have to.'

'Don't be ridiculous. You don't have to.'

'Listen, Sheila. It works. Looking back the evidence is incontrovertible. Now I've found him again. It's going to be all right. It's all going to be all right. Don't cry.'

'How can you tell me not to cry? You spend weeks wandering around looking like a zombie, drinking, coming home late. You put me in hospital, then you take me out again, then I have to go in again. Now, right at the last moment, you expect me to call it off. And you come out with all this stuff . . . these stories . . . Hell, Alistair.' She touched his cheek.

'They're not stories.'

'Oh no?'

They sat opposite each other in the small, white room groping for that increasingly narrow isthmus of common ground.

'You're serious, aren't you?'

'Yes – yes I am.'

'See a psychiatrist.'

'I don't need a psychiatrist. You said I should have told you about Spears when all that happened. You're right. I should have. Maybe I don't share enough. So now I'm telling you about Dhangi. I don't expect you to believe it straight away. I just need a bit more time. For proof. Say five more days. You'll give me that, won't you?'

They contemplated each other in silence. 'Yes, I'll give you that,' she said at last, as if agreeing to give clothes to a jumble sale. He realized that their final point of contact, her faith in him, had, for the moment, vanished. There was no more to be said.

Kingsley drove home tortured by self-doubt. He slept fitfully and awoke the next morning drenched in sweat. Unable to concentrate on his work, he cut short the morning clinic in order to visit Sheila during the lunch hour.

He stopped at the top of Leith Walk and bought two dozen pink roses from Rankin's. It struck him again as he climbed back into the car that shop assistants no longer treated him with the deference he had once commanded. Something made him accelerate as he approached the Infirmary. He left the car parked askew in the hospital car park and almost forgot Sheila's flowers in his haste. Inside the hospital he virtually ran up the staircase to the second floor.

The main surgical corridor stretched the length of the building. Kingsley hurried along it, swinging the flowers, now slowing to take breath, now breaking into a trot. On both sides of him there sped past the huge black boards which bore, in gold script, the names of those who had once donated money to the hospital. Kingsley turned into the ward.

As he passed the nursing office the small, pointed sister called out to him. Kingsley ignored her. He entered Sheila's room. It was empty. He almost collided with the sister on his way out. 'Where's my wife?' he demanded.

'Ah, Mr Kingsley.'

'Don't "Ah, Mr Kingsley" me. Where the hell is she?'

'She's gone to theatre. They'll be starting about now.'

'What the hell do you mean she's gone to theatre?'

'For the operation, Mr Kingsley.'

'She's not having a bloody operation. Which theatre?'

'Mr Kingsley. Do have a seat. Mr Cullen asked me to tell you

131

that he and Mrs Kingsley had discussed the matter, feeling it better . . .'

'Which theatre?'

'Shall I ring them?' she asked coolly.

'Just stop being so damned pompous and tell me where they are.'

The alabaster reddened. 'Orthopaedics C,' she said. 'You're too late.'

The roses fell at her feet. Kingsley slammed through the swing doors, rushed into the lunch trolley and tore off down the corridor. He took the great spiral staircase three steps at a time, dodging nurses who climbed towards him, his leather soles skidding on the mosaic steps.

A red light outside the orthopaedic suite illuminated the sign: *Sterile Corridor – No Entry*. Kingsley left the swing doors thrashing behind him. He burst through the sterile changing area to emerge, panting, in a shiny corridor. Two of the theatres were empty. There was activity in a third. A voice called. 'Gown, Mr Kingsley!'

Sheila lay unconscious on the anaesthetic trolley. He didn't recognize the anaesthetist. A startled charge-nurse dropped a bottle of surgical spirit. It skidded, ringing around his feet.

'Switch that off,' he said.

'You can't,' the anaesthetist began, but Kingsley already had.

He turned the oxygen on full. Then pushed open the doors to the operating room.

'Tony,' he said.

Cullen looked up. He was standing in his long green gown, gloved hands folded, Christ-like across his chest.

'What are you doing here?' he asked.

'What the hell d'you think I'm doing here?'

Like figures in a room at Pompeii, the registrar, the anaesthetic assistant, the scrub nurse and the floor nurses stood, lignified, where he had interrupted them.

Cullen pulled down his mask and peeled off his gloves. 'Let's take a break for lunch.' He followed Kingsley out.

The anaesthetist was bending over Sheila. She was retching and moving her arms.

There was a single nurse in the rest room. She looked at Cullen's face and left quickly. When the door closed Kingsley turned on him.

'You were going to go on and amputate.'

'Sheila asked me to. She signed the consent form. It's her decision.'

'It was your bloody decision, Tony.'

'Yes, it was my decision too.'

Cullen stood before him, immobile as a crag.

'I only asked for five days, Tony.'

'Five days for what? Don't tell me you've unearthed some new cure.' Cullen snorted. 'So what is it? Injections, magic potions, prayer? Come on, man. You can't be serious. If I suspected for one minute that you had any chance of coming up with a viable alternative I'd give you all the time in the world. But I don't think you've got anything up your sleeve, nothing, and I don't want to see you continuing to torture yourself.'

'It's my wife.'

'She's *my* patient, Alistair.'

'Does that give you the right to disregard my opinion?'

Cullen was slowly unlacing his gown. 'I don't think your opinion is valid right at the moment, Alistair.'

'You think I'm going to pieces.'

'Not just me, Alistair. When was the last time you looked at yourself in a mirror?'

Kingsley ran a hand over his chin. He had not shaved that morning.

'Look,' Cullen continued, 'like I said before – if this happened to my wife I'd be up the wall. I wouldn't trust myself with the necessary clinical judgement. I'd leave it to a more objective practitioner. You remember Louther?'

Yes, he remembered Louther. Louther had been a vascular surgeon – a renowned expert, not just locally but internationally. His teaching seminars had always been crammed. When his wife developed swelling of the aorta he had insisted on repairing it himself. Through no fault of his own the graft broke down and she died post-operatively of massive internal haemorrhage. Louther had blamed himself. He retired from active work. Two months later he shot himself.

'Five more days,' said Kingsley.

'Last time it was four more weeks.'

'That's a decision, not a request.'

'What do you want me to do?'

'Just X-ray that leg in five days' time. If the cancer's still there you can amputate.'

'What do you mean, "If the cancer is still there?" Are you planning to treat her?'

'I already have.'

Cullen exhaled noisily. 'Don't crack, Alistair. You're one of the best.'

Then he left.

16

Anthony Cullen folded his arms across his chest and pushed back on the hind legs of his chair. The bent wood creaked under his weight. A thin line of bright light transected his body, escaping from the viewing screen between the two X-rays he had clipped there. Sheila Kingsley's femur, one week before her aborted operation and four days after. Undeniably the appearance had changed. Where once had been the lobulated mass of cancer there was now nothing – a black hole, more regular in contour and already lined with a thin perimeter of opaque regenerative tissue. Anthony Cullen stuck both thumbs in his waistband and drummed the free digits on his bladder. For the third time he checked the name and date. Then he pushed back again, legs straight, grey chin pressed on his chest. After a while he switched off the viewing screen and crossed the corridor to Sheila Kingsley's room.

'I've been looking at your X-rays.'

She had put some lipstick on. Perverse as it seemed, she looked better already. She had not required pethidine for three days now and her pupils had become large and bright again.

'Well . . . ?'

He sat diagonally on the edge of her bed.

'Strangely enough. Your cancer doesn't look so bad.'

'I feel better.'

Cullen propped himself on one arm. 'Listen, Sheila, all this hooha Alistair was coming out with about being able to treat you himself. It's all nonsense isn't it?'

She shrugged.

'He didn't give you any capsules, or pills or anything, no

injections, no special drinks? Nothing which might have made you get better?'

'You mean I am?'

'That's the way it seems – despite all my predictions.'

A big smile tugged at her mouth. Cullen watched it grudgingly.

'Aren't you pleased too?' she asked him.

'Confused.'

'Do you feel cheated?'

'Cheated? God no. It's tremendous news. You don't think I was looking forward to cutting your leg off.'

'I don't know, were you? I mean I know it's awful and all that, but you enjoy it don't you. Having to do terrible things to people. That's all part of the thrill? No? Being bloody ruthless. If Alistair could treat all his patients without cutting he'd be desolate.'

He patted her leg. 'I can see your critical faculties are working. Maybe we should sedate you again.'

Back in the ward office he phoned down to Leith. He caught Kingsley in Barton ward at the beginning of a round. 'Alistair, I have an apology to make . . .'

'For God's sake, Tony, you've not . . .'

'Keep your hair on. I wouldn't dream of doing anything to Sheila now without your consent.'

There was a pause. 'I'm sorry,' said Kingsley quietly.

'Forget it.'

'It's just that . . .'

'All right, man,' said Cullen. "The fact is I've just reviewed Sheila's X-rays. I don't know how to account for it, but today's film shows definite signs of remission.'

Another silence. Kingsley cleared his throat. On the other end of the phone, Cullen mistook the sound for ironic laughter.

'That's the first time I've heard you laugh in a long while.'

Kingsley spoke with difficulty. 'It's the first time I've had something to laugh about.'

'Care to share the joke?' Cullen asked.

'What?'

'Tell me how you explain this.'

Kingsley faltered. Incredibly he had not prepared himself for this kind of question. Perhaps he had never wholly believed until now. 'Actually,' he said, 'I'm as surprised as you are. I was . . . It was nothing. I was acting on a hunch . . . that she would respond to chemotherapy.'

'We almost always see a gradual response over the first three weeks. I'd already assumed this tumour was unresponsive to drugs.'

'So had I,' said Kingsley.

'You've got me wondering if maybe you slipped her the magic potion.'

'I thought you didn't believe in magic, Tony.'

'I didn't yesterday.'

Alone in Sister McReady's cramped nursing station, Kingsley inspected his own fingertips.

'Seriously, Alistair,' Cullen was saying, 'you've not . . . you've not intervened in any other way?'

'No.'

'I can't help wondering how you were so adamant we shouldn't operate . . .'

'I told you,' Kingsley said. 'It was just a hunch.' As a man who had hitherto shared Cullen's pragmatic approach to life, Kingsley was embarrassingly aware of the thinness of this excuse. Cullen ploughed through it.

'I was thinking about your research down there, poor old Mukesh's project. Had he come up with anything?'

'Nothing,' Kingsley insisted.

'Some analogue of that stuff – interferon. They had some early success with osteogenic sarcoma.'

'Listen Tony, there's nothing like that.'

'OK. Don't get steamed up. I'm just saying I'd want to be told.'

'Well I'm telling you,' said Kingsley. 'You don't think if I'd stumbled on some fantastic panacea I'd be keeping it to myself.'

'There might be a case for it,' said Cullen pointedly. He paused. 'You can appreciate my concern; I need to know what my patient's treatment is.'

'She's getting what you're giving her.'

'Nothing else?'

'Nothing. Believe me.'

'That's all I wanted to know,' said Cullen.

Kingsley hung up, then stood in the cramped office and looked out over the darkening car park, as he had stood fifteen years ago as a young consultant on his first visit to the ward; as he had stood many times since, discussing cases, phoning, arguing the toss with McReady. All the years of experience had done nothing to prepare him for what he now faced. He steadied himself momentarily against the filing cabinet, rubbed his eyes, replaced his glasses, then stepped out of the nursing station.

As Kingsley rejoined the ward round, Jennings was instructing the houseman on the management of an intravenous feeding routine. It was Jennings's speciality; Kingsley therefore had nothing to add and his blank detachment went unnoticed. There now remained little doubt in his mind that he, Alistair Kingsley, was the only man in the world who could offer a cure for otherwise terminal cancer. As Cullen himself had suggested, there was a strong case for keeping this secret dark. And he had only guessed a fragment of the truth.

In the unseasonal heat of the ward Kingsley sweated. Sheila's recovery had immediately aroused Cullen's suspicions. It could not fail to ignite speculation elsewhere. For a moment Kingsley entertained the idea of phoning Cullen and asking him to suppress the report. But he realized now that he had already tested Tony Cullen's loyalty to breaking point. Besides, it was already too late to intervene – Sheila's films would already have been processed in the radiography department. From there the news of her apparent remission would have begun its malignant spread through the Infirmary. There was no way he could halt it.

'Mrs Grant,' said the houseman, 'for ligation of veins.'

'Hello, Mrs Grant,' said Jennings. Looking up he perceived that their consultant was still not completely with them. Jennings had admired, and still admired, his boss enormously but he was worried by Kingsley's recent demeanour. Over the past couple of months Jennings had begun to suspect that he had hitherto widely underestimated the stresses to which further promotion might expose him.

Anyway, if the old man wouldn't take a rest he could at least dream on his feet for a while.

Kingsley continued to study the floor. This gift, if gift it was, threw all his previous values into disarray. His justification for the long hours he worked had always been something to do with his uniqueness – the idea that his special skills carried with them a debt to society. But to what extent was he indebted? To the limit of his ability? Did then a limitless ability to cure imply a limitless obligation to society?

'Mr Kingsley.'

And for what rewards? As Kingsley saw it, the power to heal did not exalt its bearer. It reduced him to a mere executive, a technician, the vehicle of some greater, incomprehensible force.

'Mister Kingsley.' It was Sister McReady's rallying call. The emphasis on the *i* of 'Mister'.

The ward round had moved on. Kingsley found himself gazing down at a middle-aged woman.

'Mrs Dalgleish,' said the houseman.

Her nightgown was parted to reveal a slack, flattened breast. Kingsley spotted the mass immediately. It had produced a pitting of the overlying skin – an exaggeration of the sweat-pores, classically caused by infiltrating tumour.

'Fine.'

'Don't you want to examine her, sir?'

'. . . No.'

'She's on your list for tomorrow, sir; mastectomy and clearance of nodes.'

'I see,' said Kingsley absently. He could now be certain that any cancer sufferer he had examined since Sheila was further living testimony to his power. But then the situation had already snowballed out of control. Saving Mrs Dalgleish's life did not make his own situation any more or less hopeless than it had already become. With a sense of impending, overwhelming disaster, Kingsley bent towards his patient. He palpated the lump, not as he might normally examine it but more roughly, squeezing and probing the mass in an attempt to cover the entire tumour with his touch. Mrs Dalgleish winced.

Jennings mistook his boss's thoroughness for diagnostic uncertainty. 'It's already been confirmed by truecut biopsy.'

Kingsley ignored him. He continued working at the lump, then moved to her armpit. There was a single bulky node in the posterior wall. Kingsley rolled it between his fingers, then searched for its neighbours.

With the first intimations of his healing touch he had worried about it on a fairly selfish level, afraid of grouping himself with the quacks and charlatans, the purveyors of groundless hope from whom the medical profession dissociated itself. Now it was dawning on him that it was not isolation he had to fear. Conversely, it was sudden and overwhelming publicity which threatened him. He had observed, in some of his more flamboyant peers, the damaging effects of popularizing their profession. And their small vanities were nothing compared with his terrifying cult potential. If the testimony of his patients should spark the public imagination, he, Kingsley, could be amplified, despite himself, to the stature of some grotesque guru figure, forced into administering, arbitrarily and unsystematically, to hordes of frantic supplicants. Isolated instances of human suffering Kingsley could encompass and alleviate. But the sheer scale of the new obligation appalled him.

'What do you think, sir?'

'What do I think . . . ?'

'About Mrs Dalgleish here, sir?'

'Yes. Send her home for now.'

'Pardon?' The houseman, utterly confused, looked to Jennings for explanation.

'Pardon me, sir,' whispered Jennings. 'That lump is definitely malignant. We need to operate as soon as . . .'

'I don't agree,' said Kingsley. 'Send her home.'

'But the biopsy . . . ?'

'Send the patient home, Mr Jennings. We'll discuss it later.'

'Yes, sir.'

From below this exchange the patient, Mrs Dalgleish, looked to Sister McReady for interpretation. But McReady's expression did not change. She watched, as she always watched Kingsley, with her heavy, contemplative stare, her jaw thrust to one side, outwardly betraying neither criticism nor endorsement of his decision. To her patients, Kingsley was God. And more than all the sophistication of modern surgery, McReady valued that illusion. Her secret anxieties manifested themselves indirectly. Now on impulse she shoved her head out between the screens and bellowed down the ward. 'Nurse Michie! Why hadn't this patient been properly undressed?' Then she retreated, poker-faced, to listen for the staff nurse's footsteps.

The round continued. Normally Kingsley's inner conflicts could be resolved by his cramping sense of duty. Indeed he was prepared, if the common good dictated, to be hounded by the public and ostracized by his profession. It occurred to him, however, that confessing to his power was not in the interest either of the public or of the medical establishment which served it.

Ideally his power should be analysed and assessed, then carefully incorporated into the known scheme of things. But seized by the public now in its crude state, it could only form the nidus for a holocaust, capable of destroying suddenly and violently the whole delicate structure of medical inquiry.

He became aware of the silence around him. A naked abdomen stretched below him. It belonged to another middle-aged woman, fatter than the first, with the silver stretch-marks of past pregnancies fanning from her pubis. Kingsley crouched low, rubbing his hands to warm them.

'What's the story here?'

'Intermittent excruciating right hypochondrial pain over two years, once associated with dark urine and pale stools.'

Kingsley examined her automatically; normal abdominal movements, soft abdomen, kidneys and spleen not palpable, no obvious masses, slight liver enlargement . . .

'When I press here, take a deep breath, does that . . .'

The patient's face creased with pain – a strongly positive Murphy's sign.

'Right. That's all.'

'Well?' It was Jennings.

'Well what?'

'Do you think it is a . . .'

'Gall bladder. Yes,' said Kingsley vacantly.

He continued to brood as he left the ward. Even Sister McReady was worried by his total preoccupation. When she said 'Goodbye, Mr Kingsley,' it was not her normal good-natured clarion blast, but a softer, cushioned tone; the tone adopted by convention by the nursing profession when dealing with the seriously ill or mentally unstable.

Dhangi stood in the mortuary, his lips moving silently. The long white plastic apron hung limply around his neck, bagging out under his arms. He was studying the corpse from its head end. It lay, neck hyperextended, with its opaque fish-eyes towards him. Cranley stood with a long knife. He in turn was studying Dhangi. They had been like this for what seemed to Cranley's reckoning an excessive length of time. He was growing impatient.

'Is there something the matter?'

Dhangi did not look up. 'Open the abdomen.'

Cranley thrust out his jaw and applied himself to the abdomen. His incision started at the foot of the sternum and ran the length of the chest and belly. It was a slow, meditative cut of precise and unvarying depth, parting skin and fat and muscle in a single sweep. Too shallow and one was obliged to take several separate cuts, inevitably shredding the wound edges. Cut too deep and one could perforate the peritoneum, damaging the abdominal organs. Cranley, lips pursed, scowling, reached the pubis. The bloodless cleft had parted slightly, shining purple at its base.

'I will open the peritoneum,' said Dhangi.

Cranley obstinately took a pair of heavy scissors to the remaining strands of muscle and transparent sac below.

'. . . Please go now, Mr Cranley!'

'It's my job to remove organs for examination, Dr Dhangi.'

Cranley placed a dour, sceptical emphasis on the title 'doctor'. Dhangi did not seem to notice. He had already picked up a short blade and was impatiently hacking around the inferior margin of the rib-cage. Cranley could no longer contain himself.

'You can't do that.'

Dhangi turned and straightened. He shook himself free of Cranley's restraining grip. The knife was in his right hand. 'Please do not forget yourself, Mr Cranley,' he said.

'Don't wave that knife around, you silly twat. Someone might get hurt.'

Dhangi lowered his hand. His cheek was twitching. The

knife hung at the level of Cranley's upper thigh. 'In this place I will now be making the decisions.'

'Twenty-six years I've lived for this hospital.' Cranley's eyes pricked from the formalin.

Dhangi stared hard at him, then abruptly returned to the corpse. Cranley's fury brought a fit of coughing, bending him double over the white tiles. When he raised his head his complexion had darkened, his eyes streamed. 'I fought in the war for people like you,' he shouted.

Dhangi half turned. He glanced down at Cranley's bad leg, then back up at the old assistant. The disparaging expression crossed his face for an instant, and was gone, but to Cranley it cut home like a blade. 'That was an accident.'

'So you say.'

'That was an accident, Dr Dhangi.'

Dhangi wheeled round, impatiently. 'They happen,' he said.

Cranley did not think to ask Dhangi his source of information concerning his leg wound. It fitted, in Cranley's eyes, with the other's moral complexion—subversion, spying and ugliness, that he should have access to the dregs of each man's life. Now he took a step towards his tormentor, noticed the knife, faltered, turned, and plunged through the mortuary doors.

For the first time in seven years, Cranley took his black coat from the peg and left the hospital early.

Turning through the back gate his lurching, irregular step took him down past the meths drinkers, past the port authority and out on to the criss-crossed plain of concrete. He passed the dry dock, the cluster of Portakabins, the bollards and piles of rope. He stumbled blindly over the rails and the irregular, pocked tarmac towards home.

Cranley lived fifteen minutes from the hospital and up two flights of stairs. He arrived at his front door without once having stopped for breath. Leaning heavily against the door jamb he clattered the key against the lock until he found the hole. When he finally staggered in to his front room the air had become thin and insubstantial and a great clamp had tightened round his chest. Cranley's temples pounded, his head swam. Heaving like a stranded fish he slumped backwards into an armchair.

Ten minutes later he managed to focus on the table in front of him. On it there stood one of his matchstick models – a ship in full sail. Cranley reached for it. It had taken him two months to build, but in his clumsy, trembling hand it crushed instantly.

In the mortuary Dr Dhangi abandoned his work on the body, leaving its limp arms folded over its eviscerated abdomen. Returning into the anteroom he quickly changed out of the apron, Wellington boots, shirt and trousers. The *dhoti* was bundled into the top shelf of his locker. Dhangi wrapped it round his loins, pulled the free ear between his legs and tucked it into the waistband at the back. On the shelf at the far end of the mortuary he arranged the gilt-framed pictures of Shiva with his consort Parvati and of Lord Vishnu supported on the black water by Shesha, the serpent king. He filled bowls of incense around the small altar, drew the blinds, lit two candles and anointed his forehead from a small pot of sandalwood paste, then he lowered himself, cross-legged to the floor, raised his head and began to hum:

> *Hansa Mantra – the sound which is inherent in all of*
> *us, born of Akshar the primordial sound which was*
> *the first cause of the universe . . .*

On the shelves around him, the steel instruments began to sing and rattle. The massive brown-glass flagons took up the sonorous, booming . .frain and the plate glass of the windows rattled in their frames.

In the rest room to the operating theatre, sitting exhausted with his face mask under his chin and the stains of iodine and blood on his theatre pyjamas, Kingsley considered the shimmering concentric circles which had appeared on the surface of his coffee.

In the mortuary Dhangi rose with no apparent effort, almost floated to his feet – a dark, white-clad figure in the incense-laden atmosphere. His eyes were turned upwards; only small slivers of pupil showed beneath his upper lids. He moved towards the corpse

> *I have been flooded with the ultimate divinity*
> *I represent God*
> *I see the guru, Kingsley, inside my eyelids*
> *In my forehead*
> *In my heart*
> *And in my soul*
> *Oh Brahman*
> *That you may flood the paleface with your vital wind*
> *Accept through me the maya of this sacrifice.*

Dhangi placed his hand in the runnels of the empty abdominal cavity and smeared his body with the foul soup of clot and bowel content. Then he stopped and raised a sliver of the pale yellow flesh to his lips.

17

It had begun as a coffee break story in the Infirmary theatre rest rooms. The witnesses to Sheila's aborted amputation were sought out and interrogated. The story was related above the hum of television in the mess and in a series of dressing-gowned enclaves in the nurses' quarters. Thereafter, Sheila Kingsley's progress in hospital had become the subject of numerous interim reports, from the Infirmary kitchens to the Douglas Calder dining room, from the boiler room at Kircaldy to the labs at Bangour. Richard Short had no need to inquire as to Sheila's wellbeing. He heard every sequence in the story of her recovery from Rhona, who heard it from a nursing friend, who heard it from a biochemistry technician. He picked it up in turn from the van driver who collected the blood and urine specimens.

The day after Sheila Kingsley was discharged, Roland Spears got his first inklings of the story. It took him four phone calls to assemble some interesting facts. At the end of half an hour he had covered a sheet of foolscap with his jottings. Around him the typewriters clacked and chattered. He tapped the Biro on his teeth and sat back in his swivel chair. To his right, out of his window, he could see the shopfront of Jenners' store. Christmas was already sneaking into the window displays. Further down the hill a wide bridge spanned the city's central valley, shunting traffic northwards towards Leith. Spears rattled the pen over his incisors. Then he put it down and, leaning forwards, picked up the phone.

The Douglas Calder switchboard put him through to west theatre.

Kingsley was in clinic when switchboard found him. He was

inspecting the results of a hernia operation. The patient's trousers were round his ankles and Kingsley's hand was all but lost in the damp groin. Kingsley was asking him to cough.

Satisfied, he straightened, took his hand to the sink and washed it.

'You can pop your trousers on, Mr Reedley. That's all fine.'

Reedley had already hoisted his underpants, like a limp white flag, to above his knees.

A nurse entered. 'Telephone for you, Mr Kingsley.'

'I'll take it in the office . . . excuse me, Mr Reedley.' He passed the nurse. She stayed behind to help the patient.

In the office the phone receiver lay on the table by the remains of a coffee tray. Kingsley took the Hunter from his waistcoat. It was half past twelve. It was a while before he recognized Spears's voice.

'I'm from the *Courier*. I'm doing a short piece on the state of play with your cancer research down at the Douglas Calder hospital.'

'Who did you say?'

'From the *Courier* – Roland Spears.'

'Ah yes . . . Roland Spears.'

There was a pause, then both men started to speak at once. Kingsley's voice won over. 'Look here. I'm all for informing the public, accurate information that is. As it happens the research being carried on by the pathology department has so far drawn a blank.'

Kingsley did not admit that Mukesh's previous line of research had, to his certain knowledge, been discontinued.

'I believe Dr McMillan at the Royal is currently analysing some of our early specimens. I'm sure he'll keep you up to date. Now I'm quite busy so . . .'

'Just one small personal matter,' Spears interjected.

Kingsley flushed. He was aware of rumours being spread around the hospital circuit, but he had not guessed until now that the stories had spread beyond these confines. Spears represented a new and redoubtable threat. Kingsley's nervousness translated itself to anger.

'Listen, Spears, you've not done much to endear yourself to me. If a personal matter means what I think it means I'd say it was none of your business.'

Behind his desk above North Bridge, Spears crossed his ankles, then plunged in with both feet.

'Your wife has bone cancer. I gather there has been some delay in going ahead with the necessary amputation.'

'Spears, I can only say that you're demonstrating the remarkable lack of taste and sensitivity which I've come to expect from your profession.'

'Don't get me wrong . . .'

'I don't think I get you wrong, Spears. I have very clear views on your sort of person.'

'I wanted to ask, Mr Kingsley, if it was not unreasonable to link your cancellation of your wife's operation with the possibility of a new therapy emerging from . . .'

Kingsley came down on that one like a boot on a rattlesnake.

'Yes, I think it is unreasonable to make that link. I also think it's unreasonable to make your living out of what are for me and my wife rather distressing circumstances. I'd be obliged if you'd restrict your speculative articles to the racing columns.'

'Can I . . .'

'No. Good-bye.'

Kingsley returned to the consulting room with his hands in the pockets of his white coat. He had said he was all for informing the public. Until a few weeks ago he had believed above all else in honesty and straight dealing, but now lies had somehow become his necessary currency – given and received. He knew, for instance, that many of his peers in the profession now asked after Sheila with false sympathy. Most of them secretly held that he had mismanaged Sheila's cancer. Cullen himself believed that the presumed response to chemotherapy was temporary, that Sheila would ultimately die as a result of delaying her amputation. Richard Short had said as much. Others of his trade either equivocated, or avoided the subject with weighed care.

But Spears was outside the tight-lipped etiquette of the medical establishment. And it was Spears, with the volatile, emotive public he represented, who was most likely to recognize the truth.

There was a small newspaper seller on the corner of Hanover Street and Princes Street. He stood over his flimsy stall wearing two coats, a scarf and a cap. He pronounced 'Evening Courier' as a word of four syllables which was translated by the notice of his stand. Kingsley halted at the lights and bought a copy. He found Spears's article on the third page.

Alistair Kingsley, Edinburgh's Cancer-Cure Surgeon, once more finds himself the centre of speculation. Reports have reached us of a recent operating theatre drama at the Royal Infirmary, in which Kingsley (50) allegedly interrupted a potentially life-saving operation on his wife Sheila, known to be suffering from an incurable bone cancer. Anthony Cullen, orthopaedic surgeon at the Infirmary, declined to comment on the cancelled operation. But he has recently admitted that Sheila Kingsley has since enjoyed an unprecedented 'temporary recovery'. Cullen (52) attributes this to the effects of a course of drugs administered in the month prior to operation. But, by his own admission, her response to these drugs had previously been poor. Is Alistair Kingsley on the verge of a world-beating medical breakthrough? More immediately the question must be asked whether Edinburgh hospitals are involved in unethical experiments on human cancer sufferers. The *Courier* investigates . . .'

The *Courier* did investigate. A tall, pimply youth appeared on Barton ward. But before he had taken more than three paces into the ward, Sister McReady had burst from her office like some fat, blue butterfly emerging from pupation. 'I'm sorry, are you a visitor?'

The reporter took two steps back. 'No,' he told her. 'I'm a reporter.'

'Aha,' McReady adopted her fighting stance, hands on hips. 'And I suppose you're responsible for that article in the *Courier*.'

'Not directly.'

'Well, listen, Mr Not Directly. If it's unethical experiments you're looking for there's none here. And never have been, not as long as I've been on the ward.'

The reporter fingered his tie. Spears had warned him to steer clear of Alistair Kingsley. He hadn't warned him about this Charybdis. 'I just thought I'd have a word with a few of the patients.'

'You'll do no such thing, they're all resting. You can come back at visiting hours.'

'Well maybe you can answer a few questions for me, sister.'

'Answer a few questions is it? I like that fine. I've been answering a few questions from most of these patients' relatives for the last twenty-four hours: "Sister McReady, is it true that cancer experiments are being performed on my grandfather?" "Sister McReady, where can we find out about the new treatment?" Two of my patients have been refusing their drugs. On your account, Mr Not Directly. And I've got quite enough to do already without having to persuade folk we're not poisoning them.'

'What *are* you giving them?'

'You can come back at visiting hours and see for yourself. It's all charted at the ends of their beds. But I'll tell you this for nothing. There's nothing there that folk haven't been getting for the last three years. The breast patients get analgesics only. All the bowel resections get Kefzol and Metronidazole. I wouldn't bother writing that, they're just antibiotics.'

'What's in those drips?'

'Water.'

'And what's that you're holding?'

'It's an enema,' said Sister McReady threateningly.

She watched his retreating figure with a snort of satisfaction. She felt she had gone some way towards nipping the problem in the bud.

In reality it had already blossomed.

18

Richard Short, legs astride on the roof of the Douglas Calder, took a great swing with his number three wood. The golf ball soared over the ambulance sheds, over the meths drinkers opposite the social security, and landed, a pinprick of white, in the harbour water. Rhona pulled her coat tighter and looked at her watch.

'Nice up here, isn't it?'

Rhona traced a finger over the skylight and inspected it for dirt.

'It's filthy.'

'That's your objection to all my best ideas.'

'You know what I wish, Richard? I wish you were half as stimulating in conversation as you keep telling me you are in bed.'

Short laughed. 'That reminds me. I've decided what I want for Christmas.'

He placed the golf club over his own shoulder and his free arm over Rhona. She gazed out to sea with the Giaconda smile on her lips. It was a long request. His moustache was tickling her ear. He was still speaking when she said 'No'.

'Wouldn't cost you anything.'

'It's not a matter of cost,' she said.

'So what's the problem?'

'Do I really have to tell you? It just sounds inelegant and uncomfortable.'

'You mean they advised you against it at Mary Erskine's.'

She smiled. 'The desks weren't big enough at Mary Erskine's, and it's an all-girl school.'

'It was just a little fantasy I had.'

'It doesn't even rise to the level of fantasy. It's rather a sordid cliché.'

Short hit the last ball. It rose off the roof of the hospital heading towards the warehouses. Then he lost it against the sky. She put a hand on the back of his neck.

'Think of something else I can give you, something conventional.' Richard Short upturned the empty bag.

'New balls,' he said throatily.

She didn't laugh. 'You're incredible, Richard, you really are incredible. You're supposed to be a highly-trained, intelligent, middle-aged man. There's poor old Alistair Kingsley, working like a devil eight till six, sometimes more, trying to run the hospital single-handed, keep up with his waiting list and fob off lunatics after a cancer cure. All you're interested in is golf and fornication.'

'Not in that order.'

'There is no order – it seems to be a continuous cycle.'

'They're two things I happen to enjoy,' said Short. 'You see, Rhona, I made this decision before I took up a speciality like anaesthetics. Medicine's not just a vocation, it's potentially an obsession. You either subscribe your whole life to it, like Kingsley does, or you allow it only discrete parts of yourself. If you take Kingsley's path you have to be one hundred per cent into what you're doing. The great reward of being a doctor is that you're in constant demand. The *problem* is that you're in constant demand. And I mean constant. Alistair thinks the harder he works, the more human suffering he alleviates. That's crap. People have a need to be ill. If you fix their gall bladder they'll come back with marriage problems, or flu, or arthritis, or God-knows-what. Give your life to helping them and they'll take it, then look round for the next sucker. You think I enjoy watching Alistair destroy himself? It started a long time before Sheila got sick. He was born with this ridiculous sense of vocation and it'll probably kill him.

That's why this cancer cure stuff is nonsense. If Alistair could really cure cancer he'd be doing it till he dropped.'

'Well, I admire Alistair Kingsley.'

'I admire him myself, but not for working himself to death.'

'It's called a sense of responsibility.'

'Fuck responsibility.'

'I suppose you do. You can't play golf with it.'

As she picked her way down the fire-escape to avoid catching her stockings on the metal, she wondered why she continued to consort with him. He treated her with none of the extravagant chivalry she had evoked in previous men friends. But then maybe she needed someone like Short to scratch her carefully manicured exterior. She thought about his Christmas present and smiled to herself. Rhona unbuttoned her coat, then checked her heels and stepped off the fire-escape into the corridor outside Barton ward. One of the porters wolf-whistled as she passed the lift. She descended two flights of stairs and crossed the great hall. She was back in the office when Kingsley returned from his meeting, opening the mail and stacking it in the wire tray.

'Anything I need to see?' he asked.

'Well, there's this – your invitation to the hospital Christmas party.'

'Can I miss it?'

'You're the guest of honour.'

'Am I? When is it?'

'Week after next, the nineteenth.'

'God. What else?'

'Just all this.'

'What's that?'

'Jesus mail,' she said.

'What?'

'Jesus mail – people wanting you to cure them.'

Kingsley considered the pile of letters. 'You've got to be joking.' He began to sift through them – typed letters, hand-

154

written letters, letters on pricey notepaper and emotional notes scribbled on the pages of cheap, lined pads, some formal, some hysterical; the basic content was the same. Kingsley riffled through the last half dozen like a fugitive spy. Outside, the traffic bayed like bloodhounds.

Rhona spoke.

He turned towards her, vacant-eyed.

'What was that?'

'I said it's just the tip of the iceberg, Mr Kingsley – you should see the outpatient clinic requests.'

She fished for a smile. He seemed to be taking the whole thing rather seriously. He handed her the letters.

'What shall I do with them?'

'I don't know.'

'Shall I put them in the bin?' she asked.

'Yes, put them in the bin.'

'Maybe you can sue,' said Rhona.

Kingsley looked at her, as if trying to recognize someone at a great distance.

'Sue whom?'

'The *Courier*, for misinforming the public.'

'Yes . . . yes, maybe I can.'

'What will you do about the clinic?'

Kingsley grimaced. 'I think I'll go into hiding.'

'Will you ring your wife before you do?'

'Sheila rang? From school?'

'From home – it's her half-day – she sounded a bit upset.'

'Did she?' said Kingsley. 'Try and get me Dhangi on the phone.'

Kingsley went through to his office and dialled home. It was engaged. Dhangi was not available either. The man had an uncanny knack of avoiding him. Kingsley left the office door open and rushed up to the theatre. As he changed he rang home again. It was still engaged, or off the hook. Through the communicating window he could see the patient, already laid out and anaesthetized, feet raised in the stirrups. Jennings was slipping sterile, green sacks over the legs.

Between each prostatectomy he rang Dhangi. There was no reply. He sent a nurse down to look for him but she reported the mortuary was locked and the labs empty. Kingsley continued with his list, trying to lose himself in the operation, peering down the long silver tube, through the patient's penis and into his bladder, watching the slim wire probe as he curetted out prostatic tissue. His mind wandered, and in the swirling flux of water and blood he saw Causeway Lane crammed with the dying, screaming for his touch. He saw his home besieged by television men and camera crews, and each time he came back to Dhangi's gaunt, furtive face.

It was six o'clock when he finished. He checked the last irrigation set and left theatre. He walked through to the dressing room, showered the sweat off his body and rang Dhangi again without success. He changed into his suit and left, head down, mind full of black thoughts. A figure projected itself from the opposite wall. He collided with it.

'Sheila!' he studied his wife's face – the strained watchfulness of all refugees. 'What are you doing here?'

She started to speak and was swamped by the avalanche of words.

'I had to come. There was a man outside the house when I got home. I let him in. Then he said he had skin cancer. He had to see you. He hung around for hours and wouldn't go. I got the police. Then a woman turned up with her son. I told her there was nothing you could do. But they're still there. Sitting on the garden wall waiting. And the phone's been ringing all day. And every time someone knocks on the door. I think . . . I think . . .' Her mouth corrugated and she started to cry. Kingsley caught her to his chest.

'Come on,' he said. 'Let's go back.'

'Not home,' she said frantically. 'I couldn't face it. Somewhere else. I want to talk to you.'

He ushered her out of the front door. William said, 'Oh, Mr Kingsley, there's a couple of folk have been trying to get hold of you.'

'What kind of folk?'

'Well, ordinary people. I couldn't say exactly, sir. I thought they were probably patients of yours.'

'I'm not available.'

There were two or three people angling for him in the car park. He hurried Sheila into the car and they converged on him. Kingsley screeched away. Voices pursued them as they left.

He skirted Princes Street, negotiating the tiered Georgian terraces of the West End. They emerged at the foot of the Royal Mile, swept round the palace gates and out into Queens Park. The road lamps hung in a fragile chain round St Mary's loch. Behind it the vast bulk of the city's volcanic crag blotted out the sky.

Kingsley slipped out from the commuter traffic and took the thin perimeter road, upwards into the hill. Sheila said nothing. Now she reached out and took his hand off the gear stick. She peeled off the leather glove and switched on the light above the dash. Kingsley removed his hand several times to change gear, to negotiate hairpins. Each time she retrieved his hand. She examined the tips of his fingers, rubbed the minute, whorled print with the ball of her own thumb, ran her own hand down the flat palmar surface, then stretched it flat and traced the creases with one fingernail. She examined the fleshy mound at the base of his thumb and inspected the tiny, tortuous veins which coursed over it. She turned the hand over. She looked at the clipped white crescents of his nails and pinched the loose, thick skin over his knuckles. She pressed the veins on the back of his hands, emptied them of blood and allowed them to refill.

They had reached the higher loch. A single pair of headlights swept round its perimeter towards them, groping round the

157

valley like the soft, yellow feelers of some ponderous sea creature. It passed. There were two cars parked without lights – city men with their lovers. Kingsley pulled off the road and stopped. 'What are you doing?' he asked her.

She replaced the glove and milked the leather over his fingers.

'Tell me why Tony didn't operate on me.'

The dash-light had gone off with the ignition. Kingsley turned towards her.

'Your tumour responded to chemotherapy.'

'I don't believe that. I don't think Tony believes that either.'

Kingsley considered this.

'Do you want to take a walk?'

'Yes, all right.'

They left the car and crossed the road. Sheila took his arm.

'When I went back for the check-up I had a long chat with Tony Cullen. He took some more X-rays. He said he'd never seen anything like it before, that it was impossible. Then he spent a long time asking if you'd given me anything; if you injected me with anything, or slipped me any pills. I couldn't be sure. I was doped up most of the time.'

'I didn't give you anything.'

Sheila pulled her collar against the cold. 'All I could remember was your coming and saying you could heal cancer by touch. Tony said I must have been hallucinating.'

'That's logical.'

Sheila was facing downhill, towards the loch.

'You forget – I don't have the dreadful encumbrance of a scientific education.'

Kingsley said nothing. They started to climb again.

'Maybe you did say it,' said Sheila, 'Maybe it's true.'

'I don't know.'

'What do you think?'

'I've stopped trying to think. There's no sense in it. But yes, I've cured cancer. I cured yours. I don't know how it happens.'

158

He paused, but Sheila remained silent '. . . I'd seen the evidence before we went to Denholm last. At first I refused to believe it. Then, because of you, I had to.'

'Who have you told?'

'No one.'

'But if you think you have the healing touch! . . .'

'Just now *it seems* I have the healing touch. It's a fantastically emotive notion. You've seen what it'll do to our private life. But that's just a fraction of the problem. I'm worried about what it could do to the whole structure of medicine. I get built up into some hideous guru figure – a vehicle for some agent nobody understands. I can't cope with the demand myself. Every charlatan in the country jumps on the bandwagon and the popular image of medicine is dragged back into the Middle Ages; ignorance and superstition.'

'But in your case it works.'

'That's not the point. Once something like this fires the public imagination they're capable of destroying me and half the medical profession to get at it. We're going to lose it in a sea of hysteria before we discover the mechanism.'

'So pretend for just now that it doesn't have any effect.'

'How do I do that?'

'Put me back on the drugs.'

Wind whistled through the rocks. Beneath them the city burned in orange sodium. And Kingsley realized fully, perhaps for the first time in twenty years of marriage, the extent to which his wife was prepared to make sacrifices for him. Indeed, he had hitherto barely acknowledged the sacrifices she had already made – art college, Malta, their plan to adopt kids – each subjugated to her love for Kingsley, and that to Kingsley's love for his profession.

Kingsley took her hand and they stood silent for a moment, in the howling darkness. Sheila reached for a strand of hair which was spidering across her face.

'Anyway,' she said, 'didn't Dr Mukesh's research help you?'

'Help me what?'

'Understand this thing you have – this ability to cure.'

'Mukesh's research never really got started,' said Kingsley, not that he had, on reflection, ever really believed it would lead anywhere. He had used it as a screen behind which he could hide what he suspected all along to be the truth. 'I never believed in Mukesh's research,' he admitted. 'I let him get on with it to divert attention from Dhangi.'

'From whom?'

'Look,' Kingsley sat on a rock and helped Sheila down beside him, 'I know this all sounds totally fantastic but I'll tell you the whole story. Three months ago a chap came to the hospital. He's called Dr Dhangi. Somehow he can control the thing. When he came to the hospital it all started. When he left the cures stopped. He came back and I regained the power – or so it seems. I don't know how he does it. The effects on my touch are absolutely genuine. I'm sure of that now. I have very little contact with the man. But he has . . . he has an effect on me.'

Kingsley broke off. 'I can sense his presence – does that sound ridiculous?'

'Carry on,' said Sheila.

'If he was to climb this hill I'd know he was here. I'd know when he was a hundred yards away.'

'What's he doing in the hospital?'

'He came as a pathologist. I've checked that. He qualified in Jalore in '63, but after that he seems to have given up medicine to become a holy man. He came over here a few months ago having specialized in pathology. He began to take short-term jobs, first in the South of England, then gradually moving northwards, combing the country, concentrating on large towns near water. Finally he ended up here. He'd found what he was looking for.'

'Namely?' said Sheila.

'A place. A temple. I can't remember the name. He showed

me a rock carving of it. It's part of their mythology. The thing is, it's identical to a back view of the Douglas Calder. And me – he recognized the scar on my hand – *I'm* part of their mythology. There's a prophecy about a healer. So he came here and somehow, I don't know how, he manages to impart this power to me. I phoned back to some of the hospitals he'd visited before this, asked them specifically if they'd noticed any unusual pathology results during his stay. Nothing. It's specific, to Leith, to me. God knows why.'

'Won't he explain things to you?'

'I've been trying to get hold of him for the last three days. He just wants to be left alone. And I'm frightened of scaring him off. He's not going to offer information about how this cancer cure works. And I know at the first whiff of his being implicated he'll be off like a shot. The secret with him.'

'What's he got to hide?'

'God only knows. The man's insane. He's totally without principles, without compassion. I think he killed Mukesh for the job.'

'No! He can't have!' said Sheila. 'Why would he want it?'

'I've got a week to find out. You see, it wouldn't stop the tide if you go back on the drugs. Ever since you came out of hospital, I've had to examine cancer patients, one or two every day. Next week they'll start coming back cured. Ten days from now it's going to be apparent that every cancer patient under Alistair Kingsley over the last fortnight has effected a spontaneous remission. The Douglas Calder's going to be swarming with reporters. I can't see Dhangi hanging around when that happens.'

They stood together for five minutes, maybe ten, watching the sea of city lights and the rushing sky above. Then the cold began to penetrate and they started down the hill again.

19

Dalgleish's story broke two days later. Someone had pinned up the press cutting in the rest room of theatre south. Kingsley took it off the board – EDINBURGH WOMAN CLAIMS CANCER CURE – over a picture of Mrs Dalgleish. The *Courier* had obviously been chasing up patients recently discharged from his care. With Mrs Dalgleish they had hit the jackpot. She had given them a story about her breast tumour being injected – her own misinterpretation of the needle biopsy. Apart from that her claims were probably accurate.

Now, as he neared the outpatients, Kingsley could hear his patients – not the muted rustling of waiting-room conversations, something more threatening, more violent: the noise of a large and unruly crowd.

Kingsley approached the swing doors and opened them. He came up against a wall of backs and shoulders. Normally the patients sat in two phalanxes of seats on either side of a central aisle. There was space between the front seats and reception and a gap between the side seats and the wall. Now, above the heads in front of him, Kingsley could see none of this, the reception area itself was hidden from view by the crowd. They filled the seats and crammed the central aisle. They were packed two deep along the walls, falling over the side seats and pressed against the public health posters. From the far side of the room, above the clamour, there came the shrill, futile remonstrations of the receptionist on duty. Kingsley took a breath and pushed forwards in this direction. He had squeezed and jostled his way to the centre of the room before he was identified. At once his progress slowed. Faces swivelled round to look at him, talking, shouting. The abrasive discord of their voices increased in intensity. He continued to push down the aisle, hauling himself forwards by the metal backs of chairs. He reached the reception desk, breaking free of the clamouring patients, then climbed on to the desk and turned back to the crowd. People were standing on seats and heating pipes to gain a better view. He tried to call for quiet but his words vanished under the hubbub. He stood up, panting, and straightened his tie. The cacophony petered out and died.

'Now listen to this,' he thundered. 'This is a surgical clinic, not a pop concert, and I aim to keep it that way. There've been some rumours floating around recently which have obviously falsely raised some of your hopes. I'm sorry for those of you who have been misled. There is no treatment available at this hospital that cannot be obtained elsewhere.'

The noise of the crowd rose like a tidal wave to drown the words. Somebody was waving a newspaper, a woman at his feet, beetroot faced and crushed against the front of the desk, was protesting she'd come all the way from Cupar. Words emerged from the chaos in the centre of the room like gobs of steel from a smelter: 'experiments' . . . 'Dalgleish' . . . 'cover-up' . . . Kingsley bawled for silence again.

'You've all been misinformed,' he yelled.

He grabbed a newspaper from a hand in front of him and waved it like a baton.

'Mrs Dalgleish received no special treatment. I have no evidence to say she has been cured. This,' he brandished the paper, 'is all nonsense, complete nonsense. I'm not going to start this clinic until anyone without an appointment has left the waiting room. If you've booked to see myself or Mr Jennings, please stay. The rest of you will have to leave.'

The tide of protestations rose once more.

'I'm sorry,' Kingsley shouted above it. 'We can't see all of you. I won't see anyone who has not been referred here by the proper . . .'

But the small room continued to boil and the majority of his words went unheard. Kingsley climbed down from the desk top, trampling on the pages of the appointments book.

'Get the porters to come and clear these people out. I'll be back in half an hour when this has settled down.'

He left the receptionist with one finger in her ear shouting down the phone to the porters' room. Kingsley pushed through to the side door. A few patients followed him across to the back door of the X-ray department. He lost them there and doubled back towards the mortuary.

He ascended the short flight and peered through the small window in the mortuary door, criss-crossed with reinforcing wire. Cranley's coat hung on the hook opposite the door. The ashtray was filled with his crushed cigarette butts.

Kingsley rattled the handle. The door would not give. He hammered with the side of his fist on the glass. No response. He walked round the side of the building. Above his head one of the windows was fractionally open. He shouted up at it. 'Dhangi . . . Dr Dhangi, are you there? I'd like to speak to you.' There was no reply from inside. Kingsley waited a while, listening for the chink of metal on china, or the sound of a footstep. He glanced nervously down past the anaesthetics, towards the car park. No one had seen him come this way.

'Dhangi!' he shouted again, and waited.

He returned to the front door and beat on the glass with the side of his fist. Descending the steps again he wondered if he could risk going back to the main entrance for a key.

There was a noise and he turned again. The door had opened an inch, revealing a strip of Dhangi's blood-stained apron surmounted by the central sliver of his face – brow, nose and mouth.

'Mr Kingsley?'

Kingsley started towards the steps. The slit of the door closed fractionally.

'Please do not come here.'

'Christ, Dhangi, I've been trying to get hold of you for . . .'

'Please stay away.'

'I can't stay away,' Kingsley replied. 'Why should I? You've got no idea what's going on. A lot of people want to know what's happening.'

'Tell them.'

'I can't tell them. I don't know *what* to tell them. We've got to have a talk. Let me in.'

Again Kingsley started up the steps. Again the door narrowed.

'Not now,' Dhangi said. 'Please, not now.'

'What the hell are you doing in there?'

'Certain rites. It is not important to you.'

'Not important?' Kingsley exclaimed. 'It's absolutely crucial.'

'Please. Not yet. You would not understand.'

'Dhangi!'

No reply.

'Will you just talk to me – all right?' Kingsley implored. 'I'll meet you somewhere, anywhere.'

Dhangi's mouth opened slightly, as if he was thinking. There was a smear of blood on his upper lip.

'This evening,' he said at last. 'I will come for you.'

Nervous and unsatisfied, Kingsley returned to the clinic. The waiting room had largely returned to normal. Two porters had sifted out the legitimate patients and were now herding a small knot of people away from the doorway.

He finished the clinic by five-thirty and returned to his office to wait.

Night. The Douglas Calder hummed. The neon lights hummed. And up on the roof the wind from the sea soughed through the ventilation shafts. In the basement the central heating throbbed. The porters' wireless hummed and crackled. The trolleys clattered and the blethering televisions filled every anteroom to every ward.

Offices occupied the east face of the hospital. All those lights were extinguished now, but for Kingsley's. In the night beyond, the caged sea lapped at the harbour wall.

Kingsley looked at his watch, then he leant forwards on his elbows again, drumming on the top of his desk. Seven o'clock.

A sound.

The handle of his room turned. The door opened and Dhangi's suit appeared, then the lower half of his face. His eyes remained obscured by shadow.

'Shall we go?' he said quickly.

Kingsley rose from his desk. Dhangi turned and left the office. Kingsley followed him. They moved swiftly down the corridor, Kingsley lagging slightly behind, Dhangi glancing nervously around him as they walked. They crossed the central hall, then Dhangi turned down towards the physio-therapy department. Halfway there he stopped and drew a key from his pocket. They descended to the basement in silence, the naked bulbs throwing their silhouettes against the opposite wall. Their shadows mixed to form a thick-limbed spider that followed behind them. At the foot of the stairs Dhangi turned again. More corridors, ending finally in a blind alley. Dhangi stepped into a long, high room to their left. Kingsley followed and Dhangi closed the rotting door behind them. A dusty bulb was suspended from the ceiling. Miraculously it still worked. They were standing in one of the many mouldering cellars that supported the old buildings, running in a dark labyrinth from Constitution Street to below Harbour Lane, maybe further. This one lay somewhere under the main hall. Aluminium heating pipes traversed its vault. Kingsley looked around him. He had never visited these passages and was amazed at Dhangi's intimate knowledge of them.

Dhangi seemed to read his thoughts. 'It is written,' he told him. 'The whole building is described in detail.'

'I believe you.'

'Then you are learning.'

'I don't think so,' said Kingsley. 'I think I've just stopped asking questions.'

'That is the first step,' Dhangi said.

'Not the way I was taught.'

'It is said,' Dhangi said as he rechecked the door, 'that there are two paths to enlightenment – *jnana* – knowledge, and *bhakti* – devotion. But in fact the one cannot exist without the other. You cannot have knowledge until you are ready to accept it.'

'I came here for some facts.'

'I am telling you.'

'Look, Dhangi, I've got two alternatives. Either I try and get to the bottom of this thing myself or I wait till someone else decides to. If you want to keep a low profile you'd be better to cooperate with me!'

The nervous tic returned to Dhangi's cheek. He plucked at the back of one hand with his fingers. 'What do you want to know?'

'What happened to Chandra Mukesh?'

'Not that,' said Dhangi quickly.

'You killed him, right?'

'He died.'

'Did you kill him?' Kingsley persisted.

'What does it matter?' Dhangi shouted suddenly. 'I am here now, am I not? You have cured I don't know how many people through my actions. One dies, several live. Is that not good?'

'That's got nothing to do with it. You just asked me to accept you. How can I accept a psychopathic murderer? Tell me that. There's no way. No way!'

'I am not a murderer.'

'Well, how would you describe yourself?'

'I am a *sadhu* . . . a priest.'

'A priest,' Kingsley scoffed. 'What kind of a priest butchers his own people?'

'He was a Bengali – a fish-eater,' said Dhangi fiercely. 'He had defiled the sanctuary of Nigambodh Ghat.'

'I eat fish. Why don't you kill me?'

Dhangi breathed out heavily. 'Mr Kingsley, I tell you that it was necessary to do what I did. Those were the divine instructions.'

'You were only following orders?'

'That is correct.'

'That excuse has a particularly evil pedigree.'

'Ah,' said Dhangi, 'but what most of you Western people cannot understand is that it is not an excuse. It is a reason. Nothing can be accomplished without obedience. The gods say to kill this man in a certain way. I kill him. They say to meditate for so many weeks. I meditate. They say come to you. I come to you. They tell. I obey. You have experienced the results.'

'Exactly!' Kingsley threw his hand up, knocking the naked bulb. The frenzied shadows leapt around them. '*I* experience the results. Which makes *me* directly responsible for your actions.'

Dhangi shook his head patiently. 'They are not your responsibility, Mr Kingsley. That is simply a figment of your own conceit. The responsibility is with the gods. You are merely a conduit of their powers, as I am merely an interpreter of their wishes.'

'I can't accept that.'

'You must.'

'But where does it stop, Dhangi? Answer me that? What else do you expect me to condone? What are you doing in the mortuary all day?'

'There are various devotions . . .'

'Don't give me that. What are you doing there?'

'I cannot tell you . . . there are certain necessary practices . . .
It is still too early . . . it was by people who misunderstood
these things that Swami Vitthalnath was murdered.'

'Do you think that's any consolation?'

'You need no consolation,' Dhangi flared. 'You are the
chosen one. Believe only that. Through you the one true faith
is reborn. When the full glory of your achievements comes to
light the glory will be the glory of my gods, and you will be
their Messiah, their representative on earth, by which the
godless ones, the *mlechcha*, may be brought to salvation.'

Through the fading echoes the pipes clacked and rattled and
from a distant, drier passage came the electric hum of a service
tug – a thin filament of reality. Kingsley clung to it.

'I'm no Messiah, Dr Dhangi. I am Alistair Kingsley. I'm a
surgeon.'

'No, Mr Kingsley. That is not what you are. That is merely
your mask in this present life. You are not this body. You are
not this mind. You are neither the sleeping, waking nor the
slumbering self. You are that which continues during sleep
and wakes up at dawn. That is what you are, Mr Kingsley. All
the rest is illusion.'

'To hell with all that,' shouted Kingsley.

'That . . . that . . . that,' echoed the walls.

But Dhangi remained impassive and Kingsley's shout of
rebellion rolled off into the muffling darkness of the passages
under the sea.

Kingsley composed himself. 'Look here,' he said, 'the way
I see it is this. You have the ability to impart something to me.
You think the religious thing is an explanation in itself but I
tell you there has to be a science to it. I want it to be analysed.
I want you to agree to be experimented on. It's possible that
people other than myself might manifest this power.'

But Dhangi was already shaking his head. 'Science,' he said.
'You are talking about science. I tell you this. Science is no
more than an imperfect religion. You arrive at certain beliefs

and immediately prove them right. By such study you can never find the truth. The cosmic truths we know by experience. They cannot be boiled in a test tube. I do not give you my gods to put them in your ovens, your jam jars. This is what called me from my study of medicine. That is what I finally learnt at the age of twenty-seven, is why I accepted *diksha*, and this is how I know.' He paused. 'I know *you*, Mr Kingsley. I know you from three or four lives back. I have brought you your destiny. Simply accept it.'

He swivelled and marched across the irregular stone floor, then turned the door handle and let himself out.

Kingsley waited, listening to the pipes, to the pulse of the hospital. And after Dhangi's quick, erratic steps had faded and died Kingsley remained staring disconsolately at the moulding concrete floor. Stalemate.

20

Over the next week it became apparent to Kingsley that stalemate was a wildly optimistic metaphor for his predicament. He was in fact overwhelmed, embattled. Dhangi remained sullen and intractable while, like a gathering typhoon, the evidence of Kingsley's supernatural ability mounted against him.

Cairney had one of his police constables stationed at the hospital's main entrance, but the task of vetoing all bona fide visitors and clinic attenders proved logistically impossible. More than once Kingsley found himself suddenly ambushed and harangued by some stranger in the corridor, until the porters, self-conscious in their new martial role, would usher them away.

Meanwhile, a local television feature presented two more cases of alleged cancer cure. The cases were carefully documented, with testimony from each patient's general practitioner guardedly supporting the claims. Kingsley's only reaction was to retreat further from the public eye, avoiding ward rounds, sticking within the hospital, to the confines of his office or the operating theatre.

Denied his quarry by every indirect route, Roland Spears decided it was time for more positive action.

Kingsley arrived at his office at eight-fifteen on Monday morning to find the door already open. He entered cautiously and turned to see a thick-set young man in a leather jacket snib the door shut behind him.

'Hello,' the man said quietly. 'Take a seat.'

'Do you mind telling me what you're doing in my office?'

'No,' said the stranger, 'I don't mind telling you that. I just felt that before the public start ripping this place apart we should have another little chat.'

The voice was familiar – Kingsley scrutinized the face – strong red hair, heavy brows and thick moustache. 'I can't remember our having met before; are you a patient of mine?'

'We've not met before, Mr Kingsley. I've spoken to you on the phone.'

Now Kingsley placed the thick Highland accent. 'You're Roland Spears.'

Spears nodded slowly.

Kingsley came to stand above him. 'Well,' he said, 'I'm afraid I don't have time to . . .'

'This won't take a minute,' said Spears, barring his way.

Kingsley considered the other's large hands and muscular shoulders. 'I suppose I can report you to someone for this kind of strong-arm tactic.'

'Frankly,' said Spears, 'I don't give a fuck.'

The word still jarred with Kingsley. He returned to his desk and reached for the phone. Spears beat him to it.

'What do you want?' said Kingsley tautly.

'Just the truth,' said Spears. 'I know you think it's the press who've dropped you in this shit but, believe me, unless the public gets some information on this thing, it can only get a whole lot worse.'

Kingsley released the receiver. He looked at his watch. Rhona would be in soon. 'There's nothing they need to know.'

'Crap,' said Spears. 'Just how dumb do you think the public really are? There's been intense medical interest in these cases. Your former pathologist, Dr Mukesh, was given a substantial grant to research my wife and five others – research which had barely been started when he died in violent circumstances. Doesn't that suggest he was on to something?'

'I doubt it,' said Kingsley.

172

Spears pressed him. 'But you think it's possible?'

'Anything's possible,' said Kingsley.

'Do you think he was murdered?'

'Mr Spears, why don't you ask the police that?'

'I have.'

'What did they say?'

'Accidental death.'

'That's what I say then.'

Spears's eyes fixed on him. 'After he died, was his research continued?'

'It has recently been suspended.'

'Completed?'

'Suspended,' said Kingsley.

Spears picked up the stone paperweight. 'Do you think it would be possible for me to interview Dr Mukesh's successor?'

'No,' said Kingsley.

'Just a few . . .'

'No,' said Kingsley more forcibly.

'He's not fallen in the harbour as well?'

Kingsley flinched. Spears was not a man to tread gently on other people's sensitivities, and Kingsley realized that to have any hope of keeping him away from Dhangi he required to tell him a version of the truth. 'As you're obviously not going to be put off, here's the situation . . .' Kingsley slowed, choosing his words carefully. 'The present line of research had nothing to do with Dr Mukesh – it's Dr Dhangi's and always has been.' He studied Spears's face to see if he responded favourably to this truth, realizing as he did so that it was, in fact, another lie. Swallowing, he continued. 'However, Dr Dhangi is . . . intensely secretive about his work . . . and has never allowed the experiments to be duplicated.' Still Spears's visage displayed neither belief nor disbelief. Kingsley elaborated. 'This pathological shyness makes the situation extremely delicate – premature publicity seriously damages our chances of success. That,' here he looked directly at Spears, 'is the truth.'

173

Spears was nonplussed: 'And I suppose you're happy with the state of affairs?'

'It's a compromise.'

'You're bloody right it's a compromise.' Spears had risen to his feet. Now he leant over Kingsley's desk, banging the paperweight on its surface. 'Your own wife has been successfully treated. There's people out there who can probably be cured as well. Meanwhile you think you can sit here playing bloody God deciding who will and who won't die for the sake of some fucking reclusive scientist who you don't want to offend.' Spears's thick index finger was an inch from Kingsley's face. 'Morally, Kingsley, I think you stink. You're playing around with something you can't handle and if you ask me you deserve everything that's coming to you.'

With that he turned and barged out of Kingsley's office. The door slammed against the wall as his feet thundered through Rhona's working area and into the corridor.

Kingsley closed the door quietly and returned to his desk. A profound emptiness had come to occupy his whole person and he felt that his powers of judgement were failing him. He knew for certain that Spears was right — the storm was breaking — it could only be a matter of days before his story was national news. Even now he was aware of the silent pressure from his local colleagues, which had somehow evolved from the silence of sympathy. They were waiting for him to act. He'd been challenged and they were waiting for the reply. The time-honoured reply, redolent with logic and professionalism which calms hysterical mothers, soothes grieving relatives and silences crying babies.

Kingsley was aware, hopelessly and finally, that he had none to give.

What could he do? He could have Dhangi arrested. But on what grounds? He could accuse Dhangi openly of withholding scientific information. But on what evidence? Dhangi's apparent eccentricity would simply compound the popular belief that Kingsley's own mind was unbalanced by recent stress. They would see Dhangi as a shabby scapegoat for his own mismanagement of a discovery vital to research. Easiest of all for himself, he could force Dhangi to leave the hospital, but in terms of the loss to humanity that last resort would still constitute in Kingsley's mind an act of historical selfishness. As he saw it now, his only course of action was to allow the situation to develop, to sit tight and try to weather the storm. With luck, before Dhangi was panicked into leaving, he might yet expose his hand. If, as was more likely, Dhangi did flee the hospital he could be legitimately pursued and questioned in connection with the research.

Kingsley was aware of the flaws in this approach – that with Dhangi's disappearance he could not be sure he would be released from the healing power; that Dhangi, once lost, might never be retrieved again; that, panicked by publicity, Dhangi could resort to further atrocities. And as for the present, Kingsley realized that his own silence could only fuel suspicion against himself, that in denying the existence of these miracles he was merely endorsing his own apparent responsibility for them. As these insights occurred so they were lost in the endless circuit of argument and counter-argument. Now, like a prisoner forced to pace a darkened cell for hours on end, he was no longer aware of, or interested in the possibility of release. More than anything he wanted to rest, to forget, to be left alone.

Two more days passed. Outside their house the plain-clothes policemen continued their protective surveillance, changing shifts every six hours, thanking God for small mercies like the car heater and thermos flask. Christmas approached – every day shorter and colder than the previous one.

Dhangi now arrived in the mortuary at dusk and stayed there long into the night. Cranley would arrive there in the morning and leave mid-afternoon. They rarely met. This was cold comfort to Cranley. His life had been founded on that mortuary and the curtailment of each working day infuriated him almost as much as the desecrations he found on his arrival there each morning. Now, having avoided Dhangi for three or four weeks, his incapacitating fury had distilled into an acid of hate and resentment.

At five o'clock, displaced once more, he sat with William in the moth-eaten comfort of the porters' lodge. A fierce coal fire glowed in the twisted grate, burning one side of his face as he scowled at the table. He swilled down another draught from his mug and drew again on the cigarette.

'I wouldn't worry yourself about him,' said William.

'I'm not worried about him. He's got to go, that's all.'

'Just ignore him, Mr Cranley. If he wants to do all the work himself just you let him. He'll get sick of it soon enough.' William leant forward on the table. His shiny serge suit took the strain. He guzzled his own coffee and smacked his fat red lips.

'It's not that I'm worried about,' said Cranley. 'You don't know what he gets up to.'

'What does he get up to?'

'He's in that mortuary all hours.'

'I've seen the light on. You know what doctors are like – maybe he's researching.'

'That bugger's not researching. I know what he does and it's not researching.'

William adjusted his waistband.

'He didn't look an over-pleasant character.'

'Never says a word. Just damned insolence. Looks at you with that glaikit expression of his. Hacks away at the bodies willy-nilly. I asked him how he'd like his own body to end up looking like that.'

'What did he say to that?'

'Didn't say anything. Doesn't bother him.' Cranley raised

his cup. The coffee jiggled against his mouth and ran down the sides of his cheeks. He rattled the cup back into its saucer.

'I mean, Holy God.' He stared at the glass. 'He doesn't even examine them any more.'

'Researching,' said William.

'He's not researching. All hours he's in there.'

'Simple then,' said William. 'He's for the sack.'

'It's no use.'

'What d'you mean, no use? If the bugger won't do what he's supposed to, he's for the bloody sack.'

'I've spoken to Kingsley,' said Cranley. 'I told him all that. I told him how he hashes up the corpses, told how he won't let me do my job. The mortuary's a pit, a real bloody pit. I told him how Dhangi lets himself in the mortuary and stays there till all hours.'

'What did he say?'

'He didn't say anything. He gave that bugger the job and he won't be told he's wrong.'

'Tell him again.' William stroked the great hairs that protruded from his nose. 'Tell him again,' he repeated. 'Mr Kingsley's a fair man, he'll listen to reason.'

'Not with this one he won't,' said Cranley, 'not with this one. Kingsley won't sack this one.'

'Tell him what you told me.'

'I have. He just hums and haws. He won't listen. He's all wrapped up with the bloody cancer cures and he won't listen.'

'Well, there's nothing wrong with curing cancer.'

Cranley was suddenly aflame. 'You can't cure cancer. It's not natural. You either cut it out or it kills you. That's the way it is.'

'Aye,' said William. And the conversation was suspended.

Cranley hoisted himself from the table and left.

The great brown clock ticked in the entrance hall. Cranley sidled up the steps to casualty. The nursing station was festooned with mistletoe. The cubicles lay empty. As Cranley rounded the corner there came a burst of laughter from the kitchen. He turned and limped down the corridor. Outside, the cold sliced through his thick black suit.

The light was on in the mortuary.

Cranley climbed the steps, tried the door. It was locked. He brought out his key. His coat hung in the anteroom. Light filtered through from the dissecting room. There was no sound. Cranley waited, listened and limped through. No sign of Dhangi.

Cranley walked slowly to the slab. He looked down at Mrs Pearson. His careful stitching of that afternoon had been slit open. The lungs had been gouged out, revealing the shiny ribbed runnels inside her chest. Dhangi had taken the heart to the dissection bench. It lay on the cork, still uncleaned, crudely macerated, as if some animal had been chewing at it. Cranley walked slowly to the far end of the room, his nailed shoes grating on the tiles. He stopped in front of Dhangi's makeshift shrine and brooded darkly over the garish pictures of snakes and demons, blue-throated gods with their houris, white lotus flowers and the pot-bellied acolytes of each shining idol. Cranley took the joss-sticks from their holders and broke them, scattering their splintered remnants on the floor. He wrenched the pictures from the wall, gathered them and ripped them across, then ripped the halves into quarters. The scraps of card fell at his feet mixed with daubs of blood and human grease. Cranley extinguished the candles and crushed them on the floor, then took each cheap tin candle-holder in turn and twisted the metal upon itself.

When he had finished he walked back to the door, scuffing through the evidence of his iconoclastic fury. He switched out the light and locked the door carefully behind him.

It was seven-thirty when Dhangi let himself back into the mortuary. On the mat inside the door something caught his eye – a fragment of a picture. He picked it up and rushed into the mortuary. A flick of the switch and the neon lights sprung into life. Dhangi clutched at the door jamb for support, then flung himself forwards, weeping, scrabbling on the floor among the fragments of metal, candle-wax and paper.

21

Sheila Kingsley stepped out of the bath, wrapping a towel around herself. She parted the curtains to check there was no one outside. No one holding a silent vigil under the street lights. No nervous stranger vacillating in the front drive. She walked through to the bedroom.

'You sure you want to go to this?'

'I'm sure I *don't* want to go to it,' said Kingsley. He was standing in front of the mirror in his shirt tails, squinting over his chin, trying to insert a collar stud.

'Here, let me.'

She took it from him, placed the stud on the dresser, lifted his shirt and wrapped her arms around his waist.

'That's not helping.'

'What's it like being Jesus?'

'Come on, we'll be late.'

She picked up the stud.

'Lift your chin.' She put in the stud and smoothed his collar.

'What's going to happen to us?' she said.

'How do you mean?'

'When people know about you.'

'Nothing's going to happen to us.'

She took off the towel. Kingsley pulled on his trousers.

'Maybe it won't come to that. What are you going to wear?' Sheila Kingsley dropped the slip over her head and picked up her dress.

'This. Can you do me up?'

*

The snow fell on Constitution Street and was sloshed and bruised from the cobbles. It settled on the statue of Douglas Calder and on the black stone of the hospital, a veil of powder, making crazy catherine wheels of the street lights. It fell across the oblong, burning windows and on the railings and on the crammed car park. As they opened the door of the car, the muted throbbing of disco music emerged from the hospital to meet them.

Kingsley ran a finger under his collar and wished he'd had a drink before they left. Short drew up as they were getting out.

'Alistair,' he said. 'The therapeutic magician of North Edinburgh. You've been hiding from me.'

'Pressure of work,' said Kingsley.

Rhona stepped out from the passenger seat.

'Hello, Mr Kingsley.'

'You can call him Alistair,' said Richard Short. 'He's not famous yet. You know Sheila, don't you?'

They were standing in the porch. William opened the front door. Richard Short thrust a huge cigar into the porter's top pocket.

'Right,' he said. 'Where's the party?'

'Straight on through, sirs.'

Rhona was wearing a medium length black dress which fitted her bottom like the skin of a plum.

The old Victorian hall had been decked up in streamers and coloured paper. A makeshift bar had been erected under the balcony. In one corner Reckless Rod's Lothian Roadshow was pumping out music. Chairs and tables had been commandeered from the canteen, restricting dancers to the centre of the hall. The old hall never looked quite at ease in this guise – too essentially sober for such frivolity, like Ned Collins, the gynaecology consultant, disco-dancing.

They edged through the tables. Heads turned towards them. Kingsley nodded vaguely in acknowledgement, but he felt remote from all this, an isolation more insurmountable than his seniority or his shyness had ever imposed.

Short was navigating Sheila and Rhona towards the bar. Kingsley stood alone on the edge of the dance floor in his own carapace of responsibility, confusion and guilt. He was almost relieved to notice McReady in some vast orange garment, trundling towards him through the dancing couples like a Cairngorm snowplough.

'Hello, sis.'

'Are you not drinking, Mr Kingsley?'

'I've just arrived.'

McReady took him by the arm, her voice low and conspiratorial.

'Well, before you get too carried away, can I just talk shop a wee moment. I got a phone call from Mrs Leslie, the sarcoma lady. She says she won't come in for her op. She says the lump's going away.'

Kingsley nodded numbly.

'You don't seem over-concerned.'

'It's party night, McReady. Can I get you a drink?'

'I'm just on Perrier water.' She pronounced it to rhyme with terrier.

'But you'll have a whisky in it?'

'Just a wee one.' McReady forged a path for them across the dance floor.

Richard Short was on his second beaker of Martini. His free hand fluttered round Rhona's black dress like a humming-bird in search of nectar. Kingsley summoned a burst of bonhomie. 'Is this man bothering you?'

'Not yet,' said Rhona.

'I'm buying for sister here.'

'I'll get them.' Richard Short leant gingerly over the bar. Its surface was already swimming with alcohol. 'Doubles?'

'Singles.' Kingsley added: 'McReady's on a diet and I'm on call.'

The music took a classical turn and Kingsley asked Sister McReady for a Viennese waltz, reckoning that she was a woman to be partnered while genteel dancing was being catered for. Two years previously he'd landed McReady for a Strip the Willow and vowed never to repeat the experience.

Three dances later, Richard Short and Rhona were still at the bar. Kingsley went to find his wife. William, puffing his huge Churchill, had finally joined the party. Cranley, always a man for the country dancing, remained conspicuous by his absence.

Richard Short picked up the bottle of Martini. 'Another drink, Rhona?'

'You won't get me to comply with your unreasonable requests, you know.'

'What's unreasonable about screwing on my office table?' he asked.

She smiled involuntarily and put a hand over his mouth.

On the far side of the room Sheila Kingsley declined a subtler offer and went to find her husband. He was standing in the side door with his hands in his pockets looking out into the courtyard; high black architecture round a black square of sky. A light was on in the mortuary.

'Something the matter, darling?'

'No.'

They danced a Gay Gordons together but Kingsley talked hardly at all. He was lost again, abstracted. Over his shoulder she could see Richard Short dancing with Rhona. Short had found the side-to-side position ideally suited to continuing his train of suggestion in her pearled ear. Rhona was laughing with untypical abandon.

'Take your partners for a Strip the Willow.'

Kingsley steered Sheila towards the tables. William, the porter, intercepted them.

'Hello, Mr Kingsley. You've not seen Mr Cranley have you?'

'No, is something the matter?'

'He just said he was coming.'

'Have you tried the Rob Roy? He drinks there.'

Richard had returned Rhona to a table on the opposite side of the hall. The gynaecology registrar found them there and asked Rhona to partner him. She declined.

'I'm very flattered,' said Short.

She laid her head on his shoulder. 'Don't be, I'm just too pissed to stand.'

Richard Short looked down at her. The fat cheek of a breast was nudging out from her dress. Short eased it back in. Rhona was tearing a length of streamer and humming a faraway tune to herself.

'What about lying?' he said.

Rhona pursed her lips. A tiny smile began at the centre of her mouth and blossomed across her face. It was the first time he had heard her laugh like this – a soft, frothy laugh – unstoppered champagne. She dabbed her eyes and touched her cheek. 'You never give up do you?'

'Only in the face of insurmountable odds.'

'I'm surmounted,' she said, dropping the streamer.

'You will be.'

Richard Short helped her to her feet then followed her round the dance floor, steadying her from behind with one hand on her bottom.

No one noticed them leave. McReady was stripping the willow with gusto, thundering down the rows of dancers like a strong wind in a campsite. Even Kingsley was absorbed by the spectacle.

Beyond the great wooden doors, the hospital corridors were incandescent with muted strip lighting – all quiet but for the hum of the generators, the soft tapping of Rhona's heels and the distant whoops and bellows of the dance. Richard Short's hand rested on her waist as they walked down the empty corridors. She nibbled his neck as he searched for the key.

Inside his darkened office a light from outside the blinds striated the walls and furniture.

Rhona crossed to the window, steadying herself on the filing cabinet as she passed. 'Where's that light coming from?'

'The mortuary,' Short told her. 'It's just across the close there. New pathologist,' he explained; 'works all night some-times.'

Rhona prised open a chink in the Venetian blind and looked out to the snow-covered mortuary beyond. 'Dr Dhangi,' she said. 'Poor old Dr Dhangi. Shall we go across and ask him to the party?'

'I don't think he'd come.'

Richard Short's hand travelled up the inside of her thigh.

'What do you think he's doing?' she asked.

'Who?'

'Dr Dhangi.'

'I don't know,' said Short. 'Maybe he's going for the Nobel Prize.'

'Aaah . . . yes . . . ,' she arched her back, 'and what are you going for Dr Short?'

'Dick of the year,' he told her.

'You're giving me goose-pimples.'

Rhona closed the blinds. In the sudden darkness she slipped from Short's grasp with the deft agility of a sleep-walker.

'Rhona?'

A laugh, then his desk light snapped on behind the silhouette of her stooping form. Rhona straightened and reached for the clasp behind her neck.

'Here,' Short volunteered, 'I'll help you with that.'

'That's not helping.'

She guided his hands away from her breasts and round to the zip at her neck, then brushed the straps from her shoulders. The thin black dress slipped to her ankles. Rhona stepped out of it then turned and allowed him to rummage through her hair as she unbuttoned his shirt. Short's breathing deepened as her taut skin burned against his. 'You're perfect,' he murmured.

'Come on, Richard, you see naked women every day.'

Richard Short disengaged himself from his underpants. 'You affect me differently.'

'So I see'.

With his hands on her waist he drew her forwards again to press against his own precariously unsupported member. 'Rhona,' he whispered, 'Rhona, Rhona . . .'

'Door,' she replied.

'What?'

'Lock the door.'

With some difficulty Short cleared his fuddled brain. 'You think of all the details, don't you?'

'Yes,' she said. 'I'm the perfect secretary.'

Her legs linked behind him as he carried her to the door, turned the key and returned to his desk. His free hand swept the stationery from its leather top. Paper clips and memoranda rained on the floor. Short moved the anglepoise onto his chair then lowered Rhona gently down in its place. Her arms tightened round him and drew him on top of her.

The casualty officer reached belligerently for another casualty card. He resented being dragged away from the party to deal with this kind of dross. He knew that with ten o'clock approaching and two patients already to be seen, the rest of the evening was written off. His first patient was a sailor with a crushed finger. In the next cubicle there was a hysterical little boy with a cut on his forehead. At a distance the cut looked as though it needed suturing and the patient looked as though he would probably put up a good fight. He had just closed the screens behind him and was about to engage the sailor in conversation when there was a rattling of the casualty doors and the sudden babble of voices. A wide-eyed nurse came through the curtains.

'Assault. Looks terrible. You'd better come straight away.'

The casualty officer followed her out, instantly recharged. Everyone got a big buzz out of major trauma. The figure on the trolley was surrounded by people; one nurse was cutting his shirt off, one taking his pulse and blood pressure. Two policemen fell back as he approached. The casualty officer looked down. The familiar face stared back at him, a grey mask.

'Shit, that's Cranley.'

His hand went to the old man's wrist: nothing. He felt for the femoral. A thready pulse was still palpable in the groin. 'What happened to his trousers?'

'He was found like this.'

'What's the story?'

'Some porter found him round by the back gate. He must have been duffed over on the way to the party.'

A nurse was bundling Cranley's shirt and black jacket into the laundry bag. A crushed carnation fell from the button hole.

Cranley's lips were parted and his eyes stared upwards at the neon lights. His chest was hardly moving.

'What's his blood pressure?'

'Unrecordable.'

'OK. Let's get an IVI. Saline to start, then Haemaccel.'

The casualty officer studied Cranley's naked form. There was a big bruise on the temple but no skull fracture palpable. The pupils were equal and still reacting. Something had happened other than the head injury to account for his present state. One of the nurses had plugged in an airway and now began to squeeze in oxygen. The chest moved symmetrically. With his stethoscope the casualty officer could hear both lungs inflating. No obvious fractures in the limbs. He pressed on the belly – hard as a billiard table. No bowel sounds.

'Where's that IV set, we'll need a CVP line as well. Put some jelly on those ECG leads. Someone call the anaesthetist and the surgical reg.' The casualty officer gave up looking for a vein in Cranley's arm and began stuffing the needle into his external jugular. Maybe the head injury was incidental. There were no bruises on the abdomen but its extreme rigidity suggested that he had perforated something.

'Somebody alert theatre,' he added, relishing his brief moment of dictatorship. The evening hadn't been a total washout after all.

The hall pulsed with disco music. The dancing had increased in vitality and the conversation in volume. Inhibitions, like the paper cups, had been weakened by wine and finally discarded. A student nurse appeared in the doorway. She cast around the sea of coloured lights with the fractured, darting movements of a hunted fox. By chance she spotted Jennings in the centre of the dance floor. Starting forwards she ran into Kingsley.

'I'm sorry,' he said. 'Can I help you?'

The nurse reddened and straightened her cap.

'I'm looking for Mr Jennings,' she said. 'Mr Cranley's had an accident. He's in casualty.'

Kingsley dropped Sheila's arm.

'What kind of accident?'

'An assault,' she said. But Kingsley was already running down the corridor towards casualty.

He burst into the resuscitation room. A young anaesthetist was already established at Cranley's head and was feeding a central line under the clavicle. Cranley was in a bad way. His skin had already taken on the glossy pallor of death. Sweat pricked from Kingsley's own brow.

'What happened?'

'Query assault.' The casualty officer slipped happily into a punchy, telegraphic synopsis, 'Comatose since arrival. Blood pressure unrecordable. Bruise on right temple, no neuro signs. Abdominally . . .'

Kingsley's hand was already there. 'His abdomen's like a board.'

'Yup. They found him half naked.'

'Have you done a rectal?'

'Very lax sphincter. Some brown liquid.'

Kingsley tapped with a finger over the liver and spleen. Cranley's abdomen was taut as a drum. 'Let's get a peritoneal tap.'

He tore off his jacket and made for the sink. These were Macbeth's, not Pilate's hands. As he washed he shouted to the nurses behind him, exorcizing the guilt and fear with a series of curt orders. He returned from the sink dripping Hibiscrub. He yanked on a pair of gloves. Someone handed him a paper gown. He crumpled it and threw it on the floor.

They handed him a beaker and Kingsley painted the abdomen. Cranley's chest movements were barely perceptible, splinted by the solid abdomen.

'Cross match?'

'Done.'

'OK, rustle up a technician and get hold of all the O negative blood we have in the fridge.'

The nurse handed him a syringe of local anaesthetic but Kingsley flung it away. He threw a couple of drapes over the abdomen and picked a scalpel off the trolley. One quick stab produced a hole in the skin just below the umbilicus. He picked up the long sterile catheter and threaded it into Cranley's abdominal cavity. The fluid that drained back was a deep crimson.

Kingsley swore.

The doors flapped open as Jennings stormed into casualty, pulling his white coat over one shoulder. A strip of tinsel hung from his hair.

'What's happened?'

'It's Cranley. His peritoneal fluid is this colour – major intra-abdominal bleed. We're going to theatre.'

The anaesthetist tapped the ECG.

'Have you seen this?'

A green line oscillated across the screen – the feeble, frantic tracing of Cranley's failing heart.

'I doubt he'd survive an operation.'

'We're taking him to theatre.'

The anaesthetist opened his mouth to remonstrate. Kingsley cut him off.

'Where the hell's Short? Someone get hold of Short. Tell him we need a consultant anaesthetist in theatre.'

He clapped his hands. Cranley, moribund, gazed at the ceiling, already beyond any reasonable chance of survival, but Kingsley was clipping back the swing doors.

'Come on,' he yelled. 'Let's move.'

Cranley's trolley clattered out of casualty, chipping flakes from the plaster walls. The anaesthetist, hurrying backwards, continued to inflate Cranley's lungs with oxygen. Two intravenous drips now forced fluid into his flagging circulation. The nurse at the far side kept a wary finger on his femoral pulse. The crashing, rattling trolley echoed down the corridors. Rubber doors parted in front of them and flapped behind.

The anaesthetist had only just transferred him to the theatre ventilator when Kingsley emerged from the changing room, gown tags flapping behind him like the reins of a riderless horse. Cranley's face and neck were already obscured by a spaghetti of tubing. By the time Jennings and the houseman arrived in theatre, Kingsley had already painted and draped the abdomen and was waiting for the anaesthetist to finish setting up. At intervals he shot hunted glances at Cranley's fingers and toes which were now a dusky blue. Sister rolled up with the instrument trolley. She began checking the swabs aloud – a slow countdown. Kingsley grabbed a scalpel. He looked to the anaesthetist, now pumping up two infusion compressors.

'OK to cut?' he said. 'Cutting now.'

His knife ran the length of Cranley's abdomen. He ignored the small bleeders which sprung from the wound and sliced again and again, down through fat, through red muscle, to the white ligamentous band in the centre of the abdominal wall. As he pierced the abdominal cavity dark blood began to well to the surface.

'Scissors . . . Suction on.'

Kingsley snipped up to the chest and down to the pubis. As he did so the blood covered his hands. 'Get in there, Steve.'

Jennings was up to his elbow in the wound, groping with one hand for the aorta. Kingsley hauled Cranley's guts out towards him, over the green drapes. Blood flooded over the edge of the table, drenching his own gown and trousers.

'You got it, Steve?'

'Yup.'

Jennings put all his weight on his one hand, flattening the aorta against the vertebral column, impeding the flow of blood below the diaphragm. Kingsley stuffed another sucker into Cranley's gaping abdomen. The field began to clear.

'Retractor, self-retaining.'

He looked to the anaesthetist, sunken-eyed.

'Have we got a blood pressure?'

'Just. It's come up to sixty since Steve compressed the aorta.'

Kingsley sweated. There was still hope, there was still just hope. He looked down at the suction jars. Two litres of Cranley's blood in the first beaker and the second filling fast. Someone was mopping the floor round his feet. The anaesthetist was pushing in O negative as fast as it would go.

'Who would want to beat up an old guy like Cranley?'

'Where's Short?' said Kingsley.

'He's not at the party.'

'You managing to hold that, Steve?'

Jennings grunted. Kingsley put his hand in the wound and

explored the surface of the spleen: no obvious tears. He moved to the liver: nothing obvious there either.

'Release the pressure a bit – I might see a bleeding point.' Jennings eased off. Immediately the abdomen began to refill with blood.

'No! Press down again!' It was pouring out from somewhere. He sniffed his hand. It smelt foul.

'There's faeces in here,' said Jennings.

'You don't bleed like this from a bowel perforation. Let's have a look at the coeliac plexus.'

Kingsley flipped the bloody coils of intestine over to Jennings's side of the abdomen. Bowel content dripped onto his hands.

'Jesus Christ,' said Kingsley.

Behind his mask his mouth and tongue grew thick, his lips dry and tacky. Sweat stung into his eyes. He began to pull the loops of small intestines through one hand. The jejunum terminated in a ragged, contused free end. Above his mask Jennings's eyes widened.

'How the hell did he do that?'

'Just clamp that, Steve. Clamp it!'

Kingsley was already groping deep in the gutter of the abdomen to the right of Cranley's vertebral column. He was up to his elbows leaning low over Cranley's bowels, gagging in the festering stench. His fingers found the caecum. Half of it was missing.

'He's lost his entire ileum.'

With mounting horror Kingsley rummaged through the abdominal contents.

'How does a man lose several feet of bowel?'

'Can't feel an aortic pulse,' said Jennings suddenly.

'VF,' said the anaesthetist.

Kingsley looked up. The ECG tracing had deteriorated to a jagged, irregular scrawl. The anaesthetist was drawing up a syringe of lignocaine. He shot it through the central line and turned to the screen again.

'No change. Do we want to shock him?'

'He's a hospital employee,' said Jennings. 'I think it's worth a . . .'

'Don't bother,' said Kingsley quietly. 'I've found the source of the bleeding. He's ripped his superior mesenteric artery off the aorta. I can put two fingers through the hole. Even if we brought him round, I can't perform an aortic graft in a contaminated abdomen.'

As he spoke the activity in the old man's heart petered out. The bursts of electrical activity became less frequent. Then smaller, then nothing. The bright green dot traversed the viewer. A flat horizon.

Jennings took his hand out of the wound.

'I don't understand. What happened to the missing bowel?'

Kingsley lifted the flaccid legs and forced three fingers into Cranley's rectum. They met little resistance.

'He's . . . someone's pushed a hand into his anus, punctured the rectal wall, grabbed a loop of bowel. Then pulled.'

He let the legs flop back on the table. Kingsley studied his handiwork.

The theatre was stunned into silence. Just a drip, drip of blood on the floor. Sister excused herself.

'Aw hell, that's sick, that's really . . .'

'I'll phone the police,' said Steve Jennings.

Kingsley turned away, slowly peeling the gloves off his sleeves. He caught his reflection in the glass of the scrub room, a tall, masked figure, soaked in blood. He held up his hands, murderer's hands. The expressionless, transparent figure floated in the glass. Kingsley stared through it.

'He was a nice guy,' the anaesthetist was saying. 'Just a nice old guy. Who would do a thing like that?'

The used swabs dripped slowly from the counting rack. Kingsley wrenched off his mask. Then he made for the door.

22

The party was over. In the semi-darkness tattered streamers still hung from the balcony like primordial creepers. Three junior doctors were supporting each other – an unsteady tripod – in front of the drinks table, singing 'When my baby walks down the street'.

They stopped when Kingsley entered the hall. His theatre clogs rattled over the red tiles. One of the doctors turned and greeted him. Kingsley made no reply. He was still sick with the horror of Cranley's death. There was no surgery for that kind of injury.

He hurried across the hall, pursued by screaming guilt. The side door was still unlocked. He closed the door behind him. The glass shivered in its frames. Around him rose the heavy architecture of the Douglas Calder, capped in snow, white on black. The mortuary was in darkness now. Above it the clear sky was peppered with stars. Kingsley crossed the courtyard. His clogs compressed the snow in the flagstones, leaving rough, black holes in his wake. On the steps of the mortuary he noticed the light that leaked from between the slats of Short's study. Kingsley hesitated for an instant, then he climbed the steps to the mortuary door. It opened. From beyond the anteroom came a faint, persistent drone – a man's voice, chanting.

In the anteroom he stepped out of his clogs. As his eyes became accustomed to the dark, a table emerged from the opposite wall. Kingsley swept his hand over the surface. He encountered Cranley's heavy glass ashtray. He shook out the stubs. His hand closed around it. From the darkness beyond the far doorway the chanting continued. Higher now. Louder.

Kingsley transferred the ashtray to his right hand. He stepped through to the dissecting room. The chanting stopped.

'Dhangi,' he said.

No reply. Kingsley forced his eyes against the darkness. Lights from the small high windows fell on something dark, moving, swaying against the far wall.

'Dhangi?'

Kingsley waited, holding his breath, every sense pricking. The sickly smell of blood hung in the black air mingled with formalin.

A tiny familiar noise: a match being struck repeatedly against the side of a box, then a choked grunt of exasperation, then the match again. A light flared. Dhangi's face was picked out for an instant, in sharp *chiaroscuro*. The disembodied hand moved sideways. It lit a candle. The small flame flickered and grew, revealing first Dhangi then the eviscerated corpse at his feet.

Dhangi was naked, his body smeared and daubed with blood. Thick gloves of blood to the elbow, blood covering his face and matting his pubic hair. Behind him the great fridge door hung open, its metal drawers ransacked, empty, to either side. Kingsley padded towards the centre of the room. The floor was cold and tacky. His bare feet encountered an obstacle. In the flickering twilight he perceived a sprawling corpse. Something cold and slimy was oozing from its middle. Kingsley choked. Two more bodies were roughly piled on the table to his right. They stank. A third was splayed over the second dissecting table.

Dhangi swayed. He turned from the light, moving his tongue in his mouth like a wakened sleeper.

'Kingsley,' he said.

Words of horror and outrage rose to Kingsley's throat and choked him. 'I've been with Cranley,' he said.

'Cranley?' Dhangi spoke slowly, as if recollecting with difficulty, some distant score. 'Ah yes, Cranley,' he repeated.

'I've never seen such a thing . . . it's . . . a horror . . . it's . . . obscene.'

'He is dead now,' said Dhangi. 'That is all, just dead.'

'Murdered. You killed him,' Kingsley shouted. 'You beat him unconscious then disembowelled him with your hands. I've been a surgeon for more than twenty years, Dhangi, but I've never seen anything as grotesque . . . as horrible, senseless, unnecessary . . .'

'He brought it on himself.'

'He did no such thing,' said Kingsley.

'He was ignorant,'

'No,' said Kingsley. 'He was a good, upright, brave old man.' He focused with difficulty on Dhangi's candle-lit form. 'And you,' he said, 'whatever else you may be, whatever powers you possess. You, Dr Dhangi, are a twisted, evil person, and I can't tell you how much I regret every having associated myself with you.'

'It was never your choice,' said Dhangi. 'It is your fate.'

'I don't believe in fate,' said Kingsley. 'I believe in responsibility. And accountability. And you're going to have to account for this, by God you will. I'll see to that.'

'You don't understand, Mr Kingsley. You have never understood.'

'I don't have to understand, Dr Dhangi. This mess speaks for itself.'

'The gods threaten to desert me – they must be appeased.'

'The gods can go to hell.' Kingsley waded forwards.

'Stop, Mr Kingsley.' There was a dangerous edge of panic to Dhangi's voice. 'You have the power, you know the prophecy . . . you must trust me, just trust me.'

'I'm handing you over to the police,' said Kingsley quietly. 'Come with me now.'

'The prophecy . . .'

'There was no prophecy. Once you're under lock and key you might be able to help with some research.'

'Research. Research is nothing.' Dhangi spat the word. The candle danced, flinging wild, leaping shadows over every wall. 'You have never realized, Mr Kingsley. You are the saviour of our religion. If not in this life, then in the next.' A wild light appeared in Dhangi's eyes. 'Yes,' he said. 'You are not yet ready. In the next life we will succeed. Come, I will liberate you. Here. Now. Come.'

There was a ringing of metal on china and a long blade appeared from Dhangi's hand.

'Put that thing down, Dr Dhangi.'

> O Shiva
> Bring strength to the arm of your fallen servant
> that he may be reborn
> that he may play by the banks of the holy Jumna
> that he may attain moshka

Dhangi's mumbling, staggering form loomed out of the darkness.

'Dr Dhangi. You're sick. You need help.'

But Dhangi was advancing towards him, lurching over the crushed and crumpled bodies at his feet. The candle disappeared behind him. Dhangi came forward, a black shape in the darkness.

Kingsley swung at him with the ashtray. It glanced off Dhangi's outstretched arm and smashed into the glassware behind. Something large and heavy fell through two glass shelves and exploded on the tiles.

Richard Short kissed Rhona on the lips and lifted his thick body from between her legs. She smiled and drew up her calves around his waist. Her eyes remained closed, one arm stretched over the desk top. Short stooped and growled and worried at her nipples with this teeth.

'Christened,' she said, hugging his head.

'What?'

'Your desk.'

'And cold?'

'Yes.'

Richard Short disengaged himself and climbed down. He was searching for her dress when his eyes hit on the golf club. He picked it up from the corner of the office and padded back to her.

He stepped onto the swivel chair then carefully placed his feet astride her head. When she opened her eyes she was staring up his legs. A small, beaming face appeared over his genitals.

'What are you up to?'

'I'm going to show you a trick.'

'I've seen your trick.' Then she saw the golf club. 'What's that for?'

'My practice range.'

'I meant what's it for now?'

Richard Short bent over her. His penis dangled towards her neck.

'The sword of Damocles,' she giggled, tugging it. Short crumpled a ball of writing paper and placed it on her navel.

'OK, stay very still.'

Rhona's knees came up to her chest.

'You're not going to take a swing at that – you're drunk, you'll hit me.'

'Come, Rhona, show a bit of faith.'

'Well, if screwing a chap on his office table isn't a show of faith, I don't know what is.'

Short laughed. 'It's nothing to worry about. I'm just going to whack that little piece of paper towards the Venetian blinds. Just close your eyes and . . .' He was trying to prise her hands from her knees when they heard the shouting, then a crash. 'What was that?'

'Someone breaking milk bottles.'

Richard Short stepped from the desk and parted the slats of the blind. Across the dark, narrow alley from the mortuary came the sounds of raised voices. One of them was Kingsley's.

Kingsley took a step backwards. Intestines squelched under his bare feet.

'There's no escape, Dhangi. They'll find out who killed Cranley.'

Dhangi stopped. He swayed. Kingsley could see his eyes, now glazed and unseeing.

'Life from life.'

'Stay there, Dhangi.'

'Death from death.'

Kingsley backed away.

'Death from life.' Dhangi was three feet away. Kingsley could hear his guttering breath.

'Life from death.'

Kingsley took another step back, slipped, and Dhangi was upon him. He raised one hand to protect himself from the knife and the two men hit the floor together. Dhangi's hand was at his face, clawing, gouging. Kingsley tore himself free and rolled sideways against the legs of the china table, choking in the thick, tacky blood and the fumes of the formalin. He made a grasp for a torso, a leg, but Dhangi slipped from his grasp like soap. The candle went out.

Silence.

Darkness.

Kingsley groped for the lip of the table and hauled himself to his feet. Nausea rose through him. He fought against it, every sense grasping for Dhangi's presence. His knees had turned to pulp. He had lost his spectacles and his eyes streamed.

'Dhangi,' he croaked.

There was a noise behind him. Before he could turn a thin,

fantastically strong arm grabbed him by the throat, dragging him backwards over the corpse on the table. High above him, in Dhangi's other hand, the long blade conjured itself from the darkness. It hung for a moment above his throat. Then the lights went on.

In the blast of white light he heard Richard Short's voice. His scorched vision cleared and, from directly below, he saw Dhangi's chin swivel sideways, then heard the shearing whistle as Short's four wood scythed through the air. The golf club swept over his face in a low, screeching arc, then the awful wooden crack as it made contact with Dhangi's mandible, snapping his head backwards.

The knife fell from his hand and rattled round Kingsley's ears. Then Dhangi's dark face crumpled out of sight.

23

The much publicised advance in cancer therapy may never now emerge from the Douglas Calder hospital. The discovery has been attributed to Dr Dhangi, the resident pathologist who died there in gruesome circumstances three nights ago.

Dr Dhangi, who has been employed in Leith hospital a mere two months, is now thought to have been responsible for the murder of his predecessor, Chandra Mukesh of Canning Close, Stockbridge, and Archibald Cranley of Kings Wharf, Leith.

'The murders,' said a police spokesman, 'were the work of a psychopathic killer. It is not inconceivable,' he added, 'that Dr Dhangi's mind was unbalanced by the magnitude of his potential contribution to medical science . . .'

Kingsley put the paper down.

He felt his neck.

'Darling?'

He smiled at Sheila across the cornflakes. 'Have you seen my black tie?'

All along the front approach to Mortonhall Crematorium the cropped grass was tipped with ice. Behind a screen of black trees the Pentland hills rose into the winter sky. Steam billowed from the mouths of the mourners and hung above them as they emerged from the church.

Richard Short put on his scarf in the doorway, took a couple of brisk breaths, buttoned his coat, slapped his sheepskin gloves together and took Rhona by the arm.

'I thought the minister did that really nicely,' she said as they walked to the car.

'Yup.'

'Poor old Cranley. Twenty-six years – can you imagine that?'

'No,' said Short.

'And then getting killed like that . . .'

'Yes.'

Rhona shuddered. 'It's grotesque.'

Richard Short opened the door of his car for her. 'Yes,' he said. 'Certainly gives a whole new meaning to getting arse-holed before the party.'

Rhona stopped. 'Aw, Richard.'

'What? Quick, hop in, I'm freezing my balls off.'

Rhona was not looking at him.

'Don't you want me to drive you home?'

Rhona's lip quivered. 'Drive yourself home,' she said. Then she turned abruptly and began to walk down the driveway, shoulders hunched against the cold. For a few moments Short watched her slim, veiled figure recede towards the gate, dwarfed by the fat green rhododendrons. Eventually, convinced that she would not turn back, he hurried after her. He caught up as the first departing car mashed past them. Rhona had stopped to blow her nose.

'I'm sorry,' he said. 'I can't stand funerals. The whole thing's so much baloney. Its a damn shame Cranley got done in, but I never knew the guy. His death doesn't affect me.'

'Nothing affects you. I feel sorry for you, I really do.'

Richard Short stood around dumbly. Rhona had not finished.

'You're completely superficial. You don't have the capacity to get emotional . . . about anyone. Any kind of sentiment embarrasses the hell out of you. You have to cheapen it with some crummy joke.'

Rhona blew her nose again. Another car passed. Short stuck his hands under his arms. 'I'm sorry, Rho.'

'I don't want you to be sorry.'

'Listen,' said Short. 'I never was too hot on sentiment, I'll give you that. But I know a tragedy when I see one. D'you ever ask yourself what made a guy like Cranley work twenty-six years in a mortuary?'

'He had a sense of purpose.'

'Balls to purpose. I'll tell you about Cranley. He got called up in the last war, just before the Normandy landings. In the middle of basic training he somehow managed to shoot himself in the leg. He spent the rest of the war in hospital. Meanwhile three quarters of his battalion got massacred on the beaches. Cranley should have been there. No one said it wasn't an accident but Cranley never overcame his sense of guilt. He got himself a job in the hospital and never came out again. That's Cranley's tragedy. He felt he should have been a martyr. When it happened it was twenty-six years too late.' He tipped her chin, 'You see that?'

'I'd rather you hadn't told me.'

'It's the truth.'

'Who wants the truth?'

Richard Short walked back to the car. The passenger door still stood open. He closed it and got in his own side, then pulled off, leaving two brown scars in the pink gravel.

He stopped opposite Rhona, leant across and swung her door open. 'Coming?'

From behind the veil Rhona, cheeks drawn, studied him in silence. A car stopped behind Short's, its engine running, steam rising from its bonnet.

'Rhona?'

'Yes.'

'I love you,' said Short.

Suddenly, behind the black lace, Rhona's mouth relaxed into a reluctant smile. 'You expect me to believe that?'

'No.'

Rhona hitched up her skirt and stepped into the car. Her door swung shut and Short pulled off.

*

When Kingsley and Sheila emerged from the church a brisk man in a sheepskin jacket was scuffing gravel back over the tracks left by Richard Short's Porsche. Kingsley stopped.

'Mr Cairney.'

Cairney looked up. He recognized Kingsley and smiled. 'Hello, Mr Kingsley.'

'This is my wife Sheila. Sheila – Detective Inspector Cairney.'

Cairney and Sheila shook hands.

'I'm impressed by your thoroughness,' said Kingsley.

'What, the gravel?'

'No. Following up the murder like this.'

Cairney laughed. 'Oh yes, that. Well, thanks, but I'm not exactly here in my official capacity.'

'You knew Mr Cranley?'

'Not really. We were members of the same church in Leith.'

Kingsley said, 'I didn't think policemen went to church.'

'Most of them don't,' said Cairney. 'I'm their Edinburgh representative.'

Kingsley smiled. 'Just your little joke?'

'Yes, just my little joke.' Cairney leant back on a car bonnet. It buckled under his weight and he stood up quickly. 'You should come along sometime, both of you. We like to see new faces at St Martin's.'

'Thanks,' said Kingsley, 'but I've never felt comfortable with religion. I'm a scientist at heart.'

'The two aren't mutually exclusive.'

'I'd prefer it if they were.'

They left Cairney to complete the cosmetic job on the driveway.

Just before Christmas Kingsley returned to the Douglas Calder and the old place welcomed him back. He felt a new affection for these blackened spires and turrets, the derelict warehouses, the scrawled gang slogans, the ripped posters and all the dusty squalor of the wrestling, the docks, the pubs

204

and the bingo. Leith vibrated. It was alive. It housed the people he had sweated over and sworn at and comforted for fifteen years. Dhangi was nothing now – a shadow, an aftertaste.

He asked Rhona to send follow-up appointments to those cancer patients he had examined or operated on since September. By careful examination and needle biopsies, he established to his satisfaction that no active disease had endured the crisis.

By mid-January Kingsley felt he had earned a rest. They retired to Denholm. Late in the second week Richard Short and Rhona paid them a visit. Rhona looked glossy and radiant. Short's pointed nose had turned purple at the tip and his moustaches had a tendency to collect snow.

He emerged from the kitchen in a floral apron, polishing a plate.

'No further trouble with that leg of yours, Sheila?'

'So far so good,' she said brightly. 'But I'm still going to follow-ups.'

'In a way,' said Short, 'it's a pity you never had the operation – could have really souped up your sex-life.'

'Oh for God's sake, Richard.'

Rhona shot him a withering look. Kingsley coughed on the stem of his pipe. 'Come on,' he said, 'get that ridiculous apron off and we'll go for a walk.'

They trudged off towards Moncrieff's Folly. The low stone bridge was knee-deep in snow. Below it the river flowed in a lattice work of Venetian glass. They trudged over Jackie's field and up the shoulder of Sickle Hill. When they reached the wood they stopped and looked back; the house and the trees around it had sunk deep into the brilliant fields of white.

Short wiped the snow off the wall and sat on it with his back to the pines. He blew out and watched his breath in the sharp air. 'Nice here.'

'Lovely.'

'How long are you staying?'

'We're going back on Wednesday.'

'Why Wednesday?'

'For the Friday list.'

'Chuck it. Jennings can do it. He'd like that. You can call him on Friday to check everything's OK and stay here with Sheila until after the weekend.'

'Maybe you're right.'

' 'Course I am. Trouble with you, Alistair, is you never learnt the difference between dedication and obsession.'

'I've seen them both.'

'So stay the weekend. Your patients will survive without you.'

Kingsley had heard the phrase used flippantly many times in the past, but now it had a comforting ring of truth. His patients *would* survive without him, just as they might die, despite his best efforts. He suspected now that he had never been the altruist he was cast as, that he was motivated purely by enjoyment of his work, irrespective of its success or failure.

In a way he was reassured by his revelation, how tenuous the association between motive and action, action and effect.

His professional selfishness usually inspired love and gratitude, which was more than could be said for Roland Spears's brand of altruism, or, indeed, for Dhangi's. Cranley had been highly moral and widely disliked for it. Richard Short, now relieving himself into a snowdrift, was entirely immoral and owed much of his popularity to the fact. In such an absurdly paradoxical universe there could be no retribution for somehow having shirked one's fate.

Kingsley smiled, gazing out over the snow-clad moor. In the distance, the small grey capsule of their cottage nestled in the snowfields.

Inside, Sheila Kingsley was returning from the window when she winced and was forced to stop. For the first time in weeks she had experienced a tiny twinge of pain in her hip.

MORE ABOUT PENGUINS, PELICANS
AND PUFFINS

For further information about books available from Penguins please write to Dept EP, Penguin Books Ltd, Harmondsworth, Middlesex UB7 0DA.

In the U.S.A.: For a complete list of books available from Penguins in the United States write to Dept DG, Penguin Books, 299 Murray Hill Parkway, East Rutherford, New Jersey 07073.

In Canada: For a complete list of books available from Penguins in Canada write to Penguin Books Canada Ltd, 2801 John Street, Markham, Ontario L3R 1B4.

In Australia: For a complete list of books available from Penguins in Australia write to the Marketing Department, Penguin Books Australia Ltd, P.O. Box 257, Ringwood, Victoria 3134.

In New Zealand: For a complete list of books available from Penguins in New Zealand write to the Marketing Department, Penguin Books (N.Z.) Ltd, P.O. Box 4019, Auckland 10.

In India: For a complete list of books available from Penguins in India write to Penguin Overseas Ltd, 706 Eros Apartments, 56 Nehru Place, New Delhi 110019.